For Finlay

J. Nathan

Edited by Stephanie Elliot

Cover Design by Letitia at RBA Designs
Cover Photo by Lindee Robinson
Cover Models Travis Bendall and Haley Jorden

Manufactured in the United States of America

First Edition January 2017

ISBN-13: 978-1542302654 (Print edition only)
ISBN-10: 154230265X (Print edition only)

For my little boy. May you always dream big.

CHAPTER ONE

Finlay

"Hey, sweetheart. Why don't you bring me a little something over here?"

I sucked back what I really wanted to say to the big oaf wearing only his shoulder pads and football pants as I crossed the locker room filled with college football players in all stages of dress. I plastered on my 'I could give a damn' face and maneuvered around the players, careful not to get too close to what they didn't bother covering up with me in the room. I extended a water bottle to the idiot.

A smug smile slipped across his face. "I didn't say I wanted water."

The room exploded with cackles and hoots of laughter.

I stifled my annoyance as I pulled back my shoulders and turned away from him like it didn't faze me.

"Hey. Where you going, sweetheart?" he drawled.

I caught the sky blue eyes of the quarterback seated on the stool in front of his locker lacing up his cleats. He looked surprised I'd held my tongue. Hell, I was surprised I'd held it when all I really wanted to do was tell the right tackle I'd come to hate—the one who'd been razzing me since I'd begun with the team a week before—where to stick his jock strap.

My eyes flashed away, seeking out my spot in the corner of the room where I waited for someone who actually needed a drink to signal me over.

Coach Burns burst into the crowded locker room rattling off the game plan for the start of their first closed scrimmage of the season. Fall semester began in a couple weeks. Football players and team staff started early, hence my presence on campus during the last few weeks of summer.

I looked out at the football players, all primed with black paint under their eyes for a battle against a local college. They sat focused on the coach's words like football was life. Like it meant anything in the grand scheme of things.

I inhaled a deep breath. I could do it. I could be there. A hundred miles from home. Starting college at a school I never planned to attend. One I never even considered attending. It was never my dream. It had always been his.

***

Cole ran across our backyard. He was taller and leaner than most of the ten-year-old boys in town, owing his athletic build to football. He played every day whether he had practice or not. And on days when he had no one to play with, in other words when I wasn't around or didn't feel like it, he threw into a tire swing our dad hung from an old oak tree in the backyard.

I pulled back my arm and tossed Cole the ball. Though a little wobbly, he reached over his head, nabbed the off-center pass, and tucked it against his side. He took off running toward our mother's flower bed at the edge of our property, celebrating when he reached it like he just caught the game winning pass in an actual game.

I brushed my long dark hair out of my face and dug my hands into my hips, waiting for his excessive celebration to stop. Even at ten, my twin's confidence drove me nuts. He was such a showoff. Rightfully so, but it still irked me. So did my friends who came over to play with me but ended up staring at Cole the entire time.

He finally stopped his ridiculous dance and turned to me, his face suddenly serious. "You throw like a girl."

My eyes flared. "I am a girl."

"Yeah." His lips pulled up in one corner. "Sometimes I forget."

I stuck out my tongue. "Idiot."

"Loser."

We both laughed as he tossed me a perfect spiral which I caught easily. Growing up with a football phenom taught me some impressive skills.

"Maybe by the time we go to college, there'll be more female football players," he said as I tossed him back the ball.

I scrunched up my face, completely thrown by his admission. "You think I'm good enough to play?"

He shrugged. "You're better than most of the guys on my team."

I smiled on the inside, never letting my brother know how much his words meant to me. He thought I was good. Cole Thatcher, football player extraordinaire, thought I was good.

* * *

I stood on the sideline under the unbearable August sun. There was no reprieve from an Alabama summer. Pool water turned to bath water, and lakes were overcrowded. So unless you were brave enough to jump into a cold shower, you dealt with the heat. And out there in the open stadium, the sun beat down like a mother.

A couple players ran over to the sideline, pulling off their shiny red helmets revealing damp hair and sweaty red faces. The once menacing black paint trailed like tear drops down their cheeks. They grabbed the water bottles I extended to them. "Thanks," the shorter one uttered, while the taller downed the contents of his without taking a breath.

They tossed me back the empty bottles. I grabbed two more from the bench and searched for anyone else looking for sustenance. When no one caught my eye, I hurried to my back-up supply in the big jug behind the bench and filled the empty bottles.

"Hey, sweetheart."

Ugh. That freaking voice.

"Get your ass over here."

I turned, eyeing the asshole approaching me with nothing but disgust. And while I had a million comebacks for his inappropriate comments, I held my tongue—at least for the time being. I needed to be there. A prick like him wasn't going to drive me away.

"Didn't you see me motioning for you out there?" he growled.

Yup. I shook my head. "Sorry."

"Well, give me a damn drink," he ordered, colder than usual.

I bit down on my bottom lip as I handed him the bottle, wishing I'd spit in it first.

He ripped it from my hand. "Coach might've gotten one with tits this time," he said to no one in particular. "But she's sure dumb as dirt."

I sucked back a sharp breath.

"Grady!" a deep voice shouted. "That's enough."

I froze, startled that someone actually had the balls to stand up to the three-hundred pound brute.

Grady's eyes lifted over my shoulder. A cold calculated grin—nearly concealed by his pathetic attempt at a beard—tugged at his lips. "This don't concern you, Brooks."

"Leave her alone," the quarterback warned.

Grady laughed wickedly before his eyes shot back to mine. "Don't get your hopes up, sweetheart. Brooks ain't nobody's Prince Charming. He'd fuck you then ditch you in a matter of seconds." Grady downed the water and tossed the bottle to the ground as he lumbered away.

I didn't turn around. I knew who Caden Brooks was. I'd known before I even arrived on campus. Junior star quarterback. His conquests epic, making his way from his home state of California to Alabama in grand-freaking-style. And his looks…well, he certainly was pretty. If football didn't work out, his dirty blond hair, blue eyes, and body people bowed down to would be gracing underwear billboards in Times Square in no time. But the last thing I needed to see was Brooks waiting for a thank you. Waiting for me to fawn all over him like every other girl.

Not a chance in hell that was happening.

"You okay?" Brooks asked from somewhere behind me.

My head whipped around, my dark ponytail slapping me in the face. My eyes locked on his sweaty face, his eyes prominent in the bright afternoon sun. "I could've handled it," I scowled.

His head recoiled, the lack of appreciation catching him off guard. "Yeah, looked like you were handling it." Of course he recovered. Guys accustomed to people kissing their asses always recovered, never letting anyone see them falter. As if on cue, his features sobered. I watched it happen. I watched him realize I wasn't worth his time.

I wasn't. Nor would I ever want to be. I hated Caden Brooks. I hated him with everything I had left in the world.

"No worries," he said. "I won't make that mistake again." He turned and walked toward the other end of the sideline.

I didn't need him.

I didn't need anyone.

CHAPTER TWO

Finlay

I stared into my mirror, applying my final coat of pink lip gloss. Loose curls hung over my bare shoulders.

Cole ducked his head into my doorway. "Finlay, you coming to my game?"

I didn't bother turning around. "I have a date."

"With college boy?" His voice took on that disgusted tone he got every time my life didn't revolve around his football.

"Why do you care?"

"Because you're missing my last high school game to hang out with that douchebag."

I pulled off my flip flops and chucked them at his head.

He caught them easily. "You still throw like a girl."

"I'm still a girl." My forehead creased, something suddenly dawning on me. "Oh, I get it. The scouts will stop showing up in droves now that you committed to Alabama."

"So?"

"So, you're worried you won't have enough adoring fans there."

He cocked his head. "I'll have fans."

"Keep telling yourself that, superstar." I turned back to the mirror, making sure my makeup was still in place.

There was a long pause before Cole spoke again. "Doesn't mean I don't want my sister there."

My heart squeezed in my chest, but there was no way I'd let him know that. "Well this sister is so over high school football games."

He scoffed from his spot in the doorway. "If you ask me, she thinks she's better than high school. Better than her own brother." He turned and walked off, leaving me feeling like a fraud. A big fat fraud.

Of course I wanted to see him play in his last high school football game. He was my twin. My other half. My partner in crime since the womb. But being the star quarterback's sister wasn't what it was cracked up to be. I was QB's little sis or Cole's sister. Never Finlay. I lost my identity as soon as Cole became a hot shot quarterback. The best in the state. And while I would've liked nothing more than to watch him play, I needed to have my own thing. I needed to be my own person. I needed to have my own life. Living in Cole's shadow just didn't allow it. So I started distancing myself from him. Blaming him for the circus happening around us. And when I said us, I meant him.

Senior year, when decisions about the future were so important, his "celebrity" had hit an all-time high, taking a major toll on me. My decision to go to the University of Tampa to major in something in the medical field took a backseat to the most anticipated answer in the state. Which college would Cole Thatcher play football for? Scouts stopped by the house, called regularly, and attended his games. And it wasn't just college scouts interested, pro scouts had been out, too, even though he wouldn't be eligible for the draft for two years. In our small town, word spread quickly. The local newspaper wouldn't keep quiet about his prospects. So the girls in our small town knew they'd be hitting the jackpot if they could score Cole.

I learned quickly if someone I didn't know suddenly wanted me to sit with them at lunch or hang out with them on the weekend, they were only using me to get close to Cole. It became such a normal occurrence, I no longer knew who to trust. Never knew why anyone was talking to me, even friends I'd had since kindergarten.

Frankly, his fame sucked. So what did I do? I made sure to suck as a sister. I avoided his games. I avoided him. Like any of it was his fault. But living in the shadow of someone else was the worst kind of fate. And for my own sanity, I put an end to it.

* * *

I glanced over my shoulder from where I stood over the sink cleaning the last of the water bottles. Grady walked out of the locker room glaring at me. He would've had to work harder than that to get me to roll over.

My eyes flashed around the nearly empty room. A few stragglers were finishing up. Brooks shoved his belongings into his bag, his eyes darting from mine as soon as I spotted him. Was he still waiting for a thanks? Waiting for me to show my appreciation for him stepping in earlier? I knew what that entailed in a college quarterback's mind, and it'd be a cold day in hell before that ever happened.

Turning back to the sink, I dried my hands. It was going to be a long season. I'd come to Alabama hoping to fly under the radar—hell, it's how I'd been living my life for the last two years. But now I had Grady on my back and the QB hating me. Things were definitely off to a stellar start.

I strolled up the winding path from the stadium toward Harris Hall, my hands pruned from water and my head pounding with an impending headache. Luckily, I hadn't been placed in a freshmen dorm.

Because, though I technically was a freshman, I should have been a junior. Taking two years off had set me back—in more ways than one.

With most students, including my roommate Sabrina, not scheduled to arrive for another two weeks, it had given me time to adjust. Time to get my bearings. Time to acknowledge the fact that I was now living someone else's dream.

My first week had been tough. Baking in the hot sun all day while waiting on expectant football players wasn't at all glamorous. If I hadn't lathered myself in SPF 100 each morning, I would've fried out there, giving me more freckles on my nose than was acceptable now that I wasn't a little kid anymore. Mom and Dad had called and texted daily. I knew they worried about me. But they had their own lives to move on with. So my decision to attend Alabama gave us all the space we needed to heal in our own way.

I flashed my keycard at the front door of my dorm, the closest one to the stadium in the village of contemporary five-story structures. I climbed the stairs to the third floor and made my way down the empty hallway. I stopped at my door, admiring my fancy artwork on the whiteboard—Finlay and Sabrina in red marker interlocking with bright red flowers. No one was going to say I didn't have Bama in my blood.

I punched in the code and stepped inside the room, dropping onto my red comforter and falling onto my back. I didn't sleep much, but the thick heat and direct sunlight I endured all day seemed to be the key. Because for the first time in months, my eyes drifted shut effortlessly. And for a short time, I could be sure my mind would remain a blank slate. With too much time on my hands and not enough sleep, the nightmares and memories crept in, stealing every drop of happiness I could muster. And for the past two years, those drops had been hard to come by.

* * *

"So…I'm leaving."

I placed another shirt into the suitcase on my bed before glancing up. Cole stood in my doorway, a backpack on his back and a suitcase at his feet. "Okay."

"That's it? Okay?"

I crossed my arms and stared at him in his Alabama T-shirt. "What would you like me to say? Go kick some ass, Cole? Enjoy college, Cole? Or better yet, can I have an autograph from the almighty Cole Thatcher?"

"Why are you always such a bitch?"

"Oh, I'm sorry for not acting the way the great Cole Thatcher thinks I should act. Tell me, what would be better?"

He stared at me, disgust filling every inch of his face. I couldn't help wondering if he was equally disgusted by my newly dyed blonde hair. My latest attempt at declaring my individuality—and a total bust. "What happened to you?"

I shrugged. "Maybe this is who I am. Did you ever think of that?"

He shook his head. "No. Something happened. Something that made you despise me so much."

"People grow up. And sometimes that means they grow apart." With every word out of my mouth, bile rose up the back of my throat, prickling my tongue.

"I don't believe you."

A car horn honked. His eyes flashed down the hallway. "Well..." He reached down and grabbed his suitcase before staring at me long and hard. With the shake of his head, he turned and walked toward the stairs.

Tears pricked my eyes as his footsteps descended the stairs. It took everything in me not to run after him. To throw my arms around him and wrap him in a bone-crushing hug. To tell him he was the best brother a girl could ask for. But my stupid pride stopped me. I uncrossed my arms and went back to packing for my own impending departure to college. I didn't glance back up until I heard the screen door slam shut downstairs. That's when the floodgates opened and sobs ensued.

I jolted up from my bed. Even with air conditioning pumping through the vents in my dark dorm room, I sat in a puddle of my own sweat. It happened often. My subconscious had a field day while I slept, haunting me with a myriad of regrets.

I grabbed my phone from my nightstand. Four in the morning. That sounded about right. Heaving a deep breath, I rolled out of bed and made my way to the shower down the hall, a necessity after one of my "episodes." Once the cold water had wrenched the sweat from my body, I threw on shorts and a T-shirt and headed out for a run. Running was the only thing that knocked the memories from my head. At least for a little while.

I stepped outside into the dark morning, the hot air forming an imaginary blockade against me. My lungs expanded on a long, deep breath as I began my slow trek up the hill from my dorm at the bottom of campus, passing the other dorms shrouded in darkness.

Once I reached the quad, I maintained a steady pace. Even in the darkness, I took in the asymmetrical trees that created a canopy around the outskirts of the grass. Blue security lights lit each corner, the only means of safety in the dark space. Unlike my younger self, the darkness didn't scare me. Nor did those who lurked in the darkness. In my world, life and its unexpected curveballs were much scarier. Much more detrimental to one's well-being.

I picked up speed, challenging myself. Competing with the internal struggle I felt being on campus. By the time I'd circled the quad for the first time, my heart rate had accelerated. I knew I could run faster. Smoother. Without gasping for air. So I pumped my arms, giving myself a push to gain speed. My faster pace created an early morning breeze against my face. I felt something I hadn't felt in some time. Free.

"What's the rush?" a deep voice asked, startling the hell out of me.

My head whipped to the right.

Caden Brooks jogged beside me, keeping pace with me.

"It's called jogging." I didn't stop. If anything, I moved faster.

"No, it's called running like someone's chasing you." He hadn't even broken a sweat and his breathing wasn't labored. *Asshole.*

"Seeing as though I didn't hear *you*, I wouldn't have known someone was chasing me." *There.*

"Well, that's stupid."

My head recoiled. "What?"

"Didn't anyone teach you to be aware of your surroundings?"

No way in hell this guy was going to give me a safety lesson at four-thirty in the freaking morning. "Yeah, I guess if they had, I could've avoided you following me."

"Following you?"

"We both ended up here, didn't we?" I asked, hating that I struggled to talk while running.

"I've gone to this school for two years," he continued. "Everyone knows it's my morning ritual. If anyone's following someone, it's you. Wouldn't be the first time a fan tried to get near me."

With my face contorted in disgust, I slowed to a stop. Did girls really fall for this guy?

Brooks' legs continued to move as he glanced over his shoulder. "What are you doing?"

"Leaving you and your ego alone," I called. "You deserve to be together." I turned and jogged back down the hill toward my dorm. I could jog on the sidewalks down there.

Caden Brooks could have the quad.

CHAPTER THREE

Finlay

"I left this side for you." I motioned toward the left side of the room as Sabrina carried in her first box two weeks later. "I hope it's okay?"

"It's perfect." She flashed a mega-watt smile. Our video chats hadn't done her justice. Her blonde hair was flawlessly curled—even after driving six hours from Florida. And her body was perfectly proportioned, the way models are photo-shopped on magazine covers. "How's it been being here alone for weeks?"

"Not bad. I know my way around campus and have had the shower to myself."

She laughed as she dropped down onto her bare mattress. "My parents are just parking the car and then I've got the rest of my stuff to bring in. It's on the sidewalk out front."

I walked toward the door. "Let's go get it."

"Seriously?"

I laughed. "I'm stronger than I look."

Her eyes drifted over the long shorts and oversized shirt covering my body.

I knew what she was thinking. She was the first person who actually seemed to notice, and for once in a long time, I felt a little embarrassed by my lack of style, especially when I knew what college girls in Alabama were expected to look like. When my life went to pieces, trivial things like fashion didn't matter so much anymore.

"Putting up with football players, you'd have to be." Her eyes jumped back to mine. "How's the football team looking?"

"They're one and one right now in the preseason."

"No," she snickered. "I meant how are they *looking*?"

I thought back to the latest scrimmage and their attitudes when they were losing. Their grimaces. Their cursing. Their anger at each other. "Better with their helmets on."

She tossed back her blonde curls and laughed. "I don't believe that. Especially Caden Brooks. That boy is fine."

Ugh. If she and all the Brooks groupies who'd been frequenting the parking lot after practices knew what an arrogant jerk he was, they would've thought differently. Luckily, we hadn't had another run-in since the quad. He seemed to be avoiding me just as much as I'd been avoiding him. I shrugged. "If you like that type."

"That *type*?" You'd have thought I dropped her phone in the toilet. "That boy is every girl's type."

"Well, if it helps, he jogs at four in the morning up at the quad."

Her brows knitted together as she stared across the room at me. "Do *you* jog at four in the morning?"

"Sometimes. I just avoid the quad. It's not big enough for me and Brooks."

Sabrina's eyes assessed my side of the room, landing on my cork board. I had a few inspirational quotes and pictures of Cole and me. "Looks like you've got your own hottie."

I closed my eyes, knowing the conversation was inevitable. "That's my brother."

Her eyes rounded, intrigued and excited. "Will this brother be making an appearance?"

Tears blurred my vision as my eyes flashed away. "No."

* * *

I rushed to the front door to stop the urgent knocking. The old hardwood floors in our kitchen creaked under my feet as I yanked it open, eager to give whoever waited a piece of my mind. To my surprise, two uniformed police officers stood there. Their stoic faces told me they weren't pleased to be there. Had that cow tipping stunt finally caught up to me?

"Are your parents here?" the taller officer asked.

"They're out back."

Their eyes wandered toward the white picket gate on the side of the house before they turned and made their way toward it.

I spun around and dashed through the house to the back door, my heart suddenly hammering inside me. My mom hung clothes on the clothes line as my dad weeded her flower beds. Sure, some had been trampled by my brother playing catch before he left for school, but my dad still wanted them to look good for my mom.

As the police officers strode into the backyard, I froze. Something told me I needed to brace myself. My mom's eyes jumped to them. Her smile quickly faded. My dad stood, his face sobering as he brushed the dirt and grass off his shorts. He crossed the lawn, meeting the officers in the middle of it.

The officer's lips moved, but I heard nothing. I didn't need to. My mom dropped to her knees and my dad followed her down, clutching her in his arms as sobs tore through her. I grasped the door frame, but my knees buckled beneath me, bringing me to the floor. As sobs overtook me, I knew with much certainty that my life would never be the same.

* * *

I hurried into the large lecture hall Monday morning, my eyes scanning the empty seats. The cap size on the class was five hundred, so I knew getting there early would secure me a seat. Apparently no one else had that concern since the place was pretty much deserted. Preferring the back to the front, I climbed the steep steps, taking a seat in one of the last rows in the center section and stuffing my bag onto the empty seat beside me.

Growing up, I'd been Cole's sister. Now, away at college, away from my small town, I could just be Finlay. I was starting fresh. And while my brother never strayed far from my mind—especially with me being part of the football team he was supposed to play on—I needed to forge forward. I liked to believe it's what he would've wanted. It had become easier now that I didn't have to walk by his empty bedroom every day. Now that I didn't have to eat dinner at a table with one empty chair. Now that I was an only child.

"Move," a deep voice grumbled, pulling me from my thoughts.

My eyes lifted. Grady pushed by me, knocking harshly into my knees as his big body moved in the small space in front of me. I eyed the empty lecture hall. "What the hell?"

"What?" He stopped, his beady eyes boring into mine, daring me to continue.

"There are five hundred seats in this room. Why do you have to choose one in my row?" Thoughts of Cole had obviously fired me up.

"For the record…" He lowered his big body into a seat three down from mine, squeezing his big butt into a seat that was way too small for him. "This is my row." He dropped his bag onto the ground with a thud.

I turned to the front of the room, pretending he wasn't there. I wouldn't allow him to push my buttons. I wouldn't give him that power. I slipped on my glasses to be sure I could see the front of the room, then watched as hundreds of unfamiliar faces filtered inside, dispersing in all directions.

"Hey, water girl."

I inwardly cursed Grady's very existence, contemplating how long I could ignore him before he began drawing attention from those around us.

"Give me a pen."

I didn't even think about it. I flung my pen at his big fat head.

He ducked as it whizzed by him. "Whoa. Haven't you learned anything from ogling Brooks on the sidelines?"

Ogling Brooks? "Screw you." I wasn't about to take his shit lying down anymore.

A cross between a grunt and a laugh escaped him. "Speak of the devil."

My eyes followed the direction of Grady's stare. Brooks climbed the steps on the left side of the room with his hand entwined with a skinny blonde's. Had I not had my glasses on, I would've thought it was Sabrina. Apparently girls who looked like my roommate were his type. I found myself watching as he slipped into his seat, pulling her playfully down into the seat beside him.

"Ogling," Grady repeated, snapping my eyes away from Brooks.

Dammit.

CHAPTER FOUR

Caden Brooks

Another semester of Psych 101 was gonna blow. It was shocking I'd remained eligible to play when my grades sucked so bad. But there I was, yet again, surrounded by mostly freshmen and transfers. I glanced around the room. Eyes were on me. It's what I expected. It's what I always thought I wanted.

Leslie's hand gripped my chin, turning my face toward hers. "There's nothing in this room you need to look at but me." When guys envisioned southern girls, Leslie was it. Blonde hair, body to kill for, blue eyes that blinded, and she was smart to boot. Forget airheads. They may have been good in bed, but try carrying on a conversation with one. That shit got old.

I laughed as my eyes did one last sweep of the room. Nearly too wide for the seat, Grady sat in the back of the room glaring down his row at the water girl sitting a few seats over. *Fucking Grady.* What was the deal with those two anyway? He busted her balls every day at practice, yet the girl put up with his shit. I'd never met a southern girl to hold her tongue the way that one did with Grady. Her sassiness with me—and the way she nearly took my head off when I tried sticking up for her—told me she was no pushover. So I couldn't fathom why she put up with Grady.

The first time she entered the locker room, her green eyes were so familiar. It was as though I'd seen them before. I wondered if we'd hooked up freshmen year. Wondered if she'd been one of many who'd invited me into her bed. And given the way she looked at me with nothing but disdain, it could've been the case. But the more I was around her, the more I realized her attitude, oversized clothes that made her look like a damn box, and that messy ponytail that sat too high on her head never would've tempted me—no matter how drunk or horny I might've been back then.

The professor stepped into the lecture hall. I half expected him to eye me with the same condescending glare he'd given me after allowing me to retake his final last year—at the dean's urging. Then I still went and failed the exam…and his class. Yeah. I know. I was every athlete stereotype come to life. But it wasn't like I wasn't smart. I learned playbooks like a fiend. School was another story.

I'd been diagnosed with a learning disability when I was a kid. So it wasn't that I *couldn't* succeed in school, it was that I struggled to succeed. In high school, I'd had loads of help. But here, even with the IEP that allowed me extended time and modified exams, it didn't come easily. Nothing but football came easily to me. And with my jam-packed football schedule, it left little time to study and fully grasp new concepts. Especially five classes worth.

Don't get me wrong. I wasn't looking for sympathy. I wasn't even looking for leniency. I just knew I was smarter than my grades showed.

Leslie's hand slipped onto my thigh. Shivers rushed to my balls. I gave her a sidelong glance, but her eyes were on the professor sorting his papers on the front table. With each passing moment, her hand slid higher up, reminding me of the things she'd let me do the previous night when my roommate Forester was out and we christened more than one of the rooms on the first floor. The girl was insatiable. And I was *not* complaining. We'd been together since March. And though I had many opportunities to test the waters elsewhere, I'd been good, keeping it in my pants. At least since we'd been dating. The majority of my first two years had been a free-for-all, and I took full advantage of the girls making themselves available to me. Not proud, just saying.

But I'd learned early on not to fuck around on girls while in a relationship. My father took off on my mom when I was ten for another woman. Seeing my mom's despair over him starting a new life with the woman he'd cheated with, well that instilled a deep hatred in me for cheaters—especially my selfish piece-of-shit father.

"What's wrong?" Leslie asked. "You just got all tense on me?"

I shrugged. We may have been dating, but it didn't mean I went all emo with her, spilling my guts about personal shit. We hung out. We had fun. We had lots of sex. Why bring my issues into it? She already knew I struggled with my classes. That was hard to keep hidden when I had to repeat more than one class. Lucky for me, she made it her mission this year to help me, taking two classes with me so when I was out of town at away games, she could take notes and catch me up when I returned. And she promised to make those sessions worth my while.

I glanced over my shoulder at Grady. The idiot was already asleep. Fortunately for the water girl, as long as he slept, he couldn't bust her chops.

Finlay

The professor rambled on for an hour straight. I tried to keep up, typing as much of what he said as I could, but when I perused my document, most of the words were misspelled and unrecognizable. College was going to be a lot tougher than high school. And my two-year hiatus waiting tables clearly didn't help.

Thankfully, Grady slept through the entire lecture, so I didn't have his antics to contend with. When the class was dismissed, I left him sound asleep in his seat. I stepped outside into the hot morning with a smile on my face, loving that the fool would wake up in either a big empty auditorium or in another class all together.

"Finlay."

I turned to find Sabrina beaming as she hurried over to me. "Hey."

"Want to grab some breakfast?"

I glanced at my phone. I had almost an hour before calculus. "Sure."

"Guess what?" she said as we began our trek across the busy quad. "I'm pledging a sorority."

"Oh."

"Why did you say it like that?" she asked nervously.

"No reason."

"So, you'll pledge with me?"

My head snapped back. "Totally not my thing."

Deep lines formed in her forehead. "Why not?"

Living with a bunch of girls you were forced to be friends with was not even close to being my thing. "Well…I'm really busy with football. And I'll be traveling most weekends…I wouldn't have time."

She considered my response for a long moment. "Makes sense."

I nodded, somehow hoping it affirmed my words.

"Well, you're not getting out of it that easily. I'm still dragging you to all the frat parties with me."

"What about me screams frat party?" I asked.

"Hot guys? Unlimited alcohol? Come on. You're in college, Finlay Thatcher. Live it up, girl."

Live it up.

Now that was a notion I hadn't considered in over two years.

CHAPTER FIVE

Finlay

Six o'clock came a lot earlier than I was used to. Two coach buses idled at the curb when I arrived at the field house. The darkened windows gave the façade that someone important rode inside. Sadly, it was just a bunch of overconfident guys making the five-and-a-half hour trip across state lines, dead set on wiping the field with Tennessee.

I didn't know what to expect. Most people envisioned wild hotel parties at night and hungover players in the morning, but I'd been assured every second of our two-night trip was scheduled for us, leaving no time for horseplay.

I climbed onto the first bus, lifting my earbuds from around my neck and slipping them into my ears. Though my music didn't play, I had no desire to deal with Grady or his comments. Luckily, he hadn't boarded yet, and the other guys were so wrapped up in their phones to even care that I'd stepped onto the bus. To most, I was just a fixture in the locker room that stood between them and a drink.

I passed the first few rows of seats filled with coaches. I stopped at the fourth row on the left beside the statistician, studying a bunch of papers in the window seat. "This seat taken?"

She looked up, her small eyes studying me. Had she not heard me?

I lifted my chin toward the empty seat. "The seat. Can I sit?"

She nodded before her attention returned to the papers spread out all over her seat tray.

I slipped into the aisle seat, anchoring my backpack between my feet to keep my bag of chocolate nearby. Cole always said I was a nightmare to deal with when I didn't get my chocolate fill. A dull ache formed in the pit of my stomach. I was traveling with the team he should've been traveling with. I was doing something he never had the chance to do.

Not having him around was never going to get easier.

I glanced over at my seatmate. Her mousy features and messy hair appeared so much more prominent in such close quarters. We'd been at practices and scrimmages together, but we'd never been introduced. She was always busy trailing the coach and spouting off player stats to him.

"I'm Finlay."

She nodded. "I know."

I waited for her to offer her name. She didn't.

Alrighty then. A tight-knit friendship may not have been in the cards for us, but since we were the only two females traveling with the team, we were going to be roommates for the foreseeable future.

Forester, one of the wide receivers, brushed by me as he squeezed down the tight aisle. I readjusted my elbow and glanced to the door just in time to catch Grady climbing aboard.

As soon as his eyes met mine, a menacing smile spread across his ugly face. One too many helmets to the face had undoubtedly mangled his now crooked nose. He moved down the aisle and stopped beside me, his big form casting a shadow in the early morning sun. "Smooth move leaving me in class, water girl. Nicely played." His eyes shifted to my seatmate. "Hey, Yvette."

My eyes shot to *Yvette* who smiled coyly.

"What are you looking at?" Grady snarled.

My eyes jumped back to him. His snarl was directed at me. "Wow," I said. "For a second there, I thought you might not be an ass."

He actually snickered before the guy behind him shoved him, keeping him moving.

Some familiar faces passed as they sought a seat in the rear of the bus. Brooks passed somewhere in the middle not bothering to look at me. The hoodie pulled over his head kept everyone out. I'd learned quickly that he mostly kept to himself, sitting away from everyone while focusing on the job at hand. Even still, I wondered how long he planned to stay quiet after the number of missed blocks his offensive line had in the preseason. Those screw-ups allowed him to take one too many hard hits. Hits that never should've happened. I wouldn't blame him for being pissed, especially at Grady. That was his only job. Protect his quarterback and the idiot couldn't even handle that.

The ride to Tennessee was long and quiet. With coaches all around me, I heard nothing more than soft voices discussing play options and defensive formations. The players were unusually quiet. I glanced over my shoulder only once, noticing most of them slept, all with headphones covering their ears. Brooks was on the opposite side of the aisle, not too far behind me, studying a binder. I assumed he was memorizing plays. It's what Cole did in his free time. Sometimes, when we were younger, I'd swipe his binder just to watch him freak out.

Brooks' eyes lifted.

I looked away, not giving him a moment to think I was one of those fans. The ones he claimed found any reason to get near him.

I was far from a fan.

* * *

I loaded up my cart with bottles and ten gallon coolers and rolled it out to the sideline. Our players, clad in white and red practice jerseys, were an unwelcome splash of color in the empty stadium, with its orange and white checkerboard end zone.

The defensive coordinators ran the defense through drills, their whistles echoing through the huge empty stadium. The offensive coordinators called out play routes to the running backs. And Brooks and his backup alternated throwing passes to the wide receivers running out-patterns. Coach Burns' voice reverberated around the vacant space as he barked out instructions, making it known that losing tomorrow's game wasn't an option.

"Hey."

I spun around. Brooks approached with his helmet in one hand and his other hand outstretched. I hurried to my cart and grabbed a bottle, tossing it to him a good ten feet away.

Caught off guard by my long throw, he scrambled to catch it.

"I guess we're lucky you're not a receiver," I said, the words rushing out of me before I could stop them.

He stared back at me, his lips tipped slightly in the corners. "With that arm, maybe Coach'll send you out there instead of me. My passes are clearly shit today."

Don't do it. Please don't do it. "Your timing's off."

His head flinched back. "What?"

"Your releases. They're just a second too soon."

His eyes tightened. A cross between disbelief and condescension flooded them. "Says who?"

I shrugged, wishing I'd kept my big mouth shut.

He continued to stare at me long and hard, clearly trying to figure out where the hell I'd come from.

"Brooks!" Coach yelled down the sideline.

Brooks' head whipped around.

"Stop flirting and get the hell over here."

I spun away from him, instantly busying myself with my bottles. *Fan-freaking-tastic.* Half the sideline had heard the coach.

More than once during the remainder of the practice I caught Brooks staring down the sideline at me. Most girls would've loved his attention. But it wasn't like his eyes smoldered when he looked at me. They didn't soften in a way that was intended to flatter—or get him laid. No. He stared at me like I was some kind of anomaly. A runt in an adorable litter.

Like I was someone who made no sense to him.

* * *

I stuck in my earbuds and leaned back in my seat, waiting for the bus to take us back to the hotel. This time I turned on my music and closed my eyes, wanting to get lost in the sounds of anything other than football.

Player after player walked by me, brushing against my arm, but I didn't stir. Before long, I heard the loud scraping of the bus door closing and felt the bucking of the bus moving forward. Unexpectedly, someone poked my arm. My eyes sprang open. Brooks stood in the aisle looking down at me, his hair damp from a shower, his cheeks flushed from the heat. He motioned to his ears, indicating for me to take out my earbuds.

I tugged them out, though country music continued to drift from them. "Yeah?"

He stared down at me, his big blue eyes studying my face. "You were right about my releases."

There wasn't a doubt in my mind why his passes were off. I'd seen Cole go through the same thing. We made it a game. Every time we practiced, he'd have to yell "one thousand" before he threw. That way he ensured he hadn't rushed it. He gave himself that extra second. And like clockwork, he got his mojo back.

Brooks stayed beside me, apparently waiting for me to say something—maybe even gloat. But I had nothing to gloat about. I spent my entire childhood playing football with Cole. How could I not point out the obvious to the guy who took Cole's spot on the team?

"You're welcome," I said, tucking my earbuds back into my ears.

Brooks took the hint, continuing down the aisle to his seat. And away from me.

CHAPTER SIX

Finlay

I now understood why ushers in concert arenas wore ear protectors. The volume in the packed stadium was an ear-splitting roar. The heat was even more intense than the previous day since the seats, now filled with fans, prevented fresh air from reaching us down on the field.

With the second quarter well underway and our defense out on the field, I finally took a second to glance around the massive stadium with its three tiers. Fans clad in orange and white filled the seats. As anticipated, a smattering of red shirts claimed small areas of the stadium—diehard Bama fans traveling out of state to see their team.

My family had traveled to countless games while I was growing up, loyally following the home team to provide support. For Cole, it had been motivation. Motivation to eventually wear the crimson uniforms that the players surrounding me had the honor of wearing.

My eyes drifted shut for a long moment, just taking it all in. It's what it would've felt like for Cole to be there. To hear the cheers from our fans and the boos from the home team's fans—all wishing he fumbled or threw an interception. Regardless, he would've loved it—every intense second of it. I shook off the thought, not wanting to shed tears in the packed stadium.

A ping of jealousy—and hatred—overtook me as I spotted Brooks seated on the sidelines wearing a headset and talking to someone up in the booth. Why did he get to play? Why did he get everything Cole wanted?

We were trailing by three with just minutes left in the fourth quarter. I was beckoned to the thirty-yard line during a time out. Fred, the equipment manager, and I jogged out there with our bottle carriers. A rumbling roar surrounded us, fans eager for the game to resume. The offense was huddled up when we approached, listening to Brooks rattle off the next play. Hands thrust out from all directions. Most of the players shot a quick stream of water down their throats and tossed the bottles back at me. Brooks shot a stream through the bars in his helmet, but he didn't stop like the others. He chugged half the bottle.

I cleared my throat, intentionally.

His eyes jumped to mine as he continued to drink. Once he stopped, he glared at me. "Problem?"

I shook my head. "I'm not the one who's gonna cramp up in the middle of the play."

His eyes flared beneath his helmet.

I turned and jogged off the field, knowing the guy was in for a rough season if he didn't smarten up.

* * *

I awoke with a start, my eyes instantly flying around the dark space. I breathed a sigh of relief. I was still in the hotel with Yvette snoring softly in the bed next to mine. I glanced to the nightstand and grabbed for my phone, checking the time. Four in the morning. That was about right. I placed it back down and rolled over, closing my eyes and willing myself back to sleep. But as much as my body needed it, my mind wouldn't allow it. As soon as I found myself in any type of silence, the memories crept in. The regret. The guilt. The incessant sadness.

I pushed myself up. Now what? We weren't supposed to leave our rooms once we were in for the night. But Coach would've had to make an exception for an insomniac with issues. Especially since he and the rest of the staff would've been asleep for another two hours.

I crept out of bed and ducked into the pitch-black bathroom, slipping on my shorts, T-shirt, and sneakers. In the hallway, I tucked my earbuds in and made my way downstairs to the hotel gym. The motion-sensor light in the dark room switched on when I entered, illuminating the impressive space. Treadmills and elliptical machines lined one wall. The opposite wall housed the free weights.

I stepped onto the corner treadmill, set my pace, and took off running. Music filled my ears as my thoughts trailed to a much-needed happy place. I tried to steer clear of the past. I couldn't allow it to veer that way. Maybe I needed to find a counselor. It had definitely helped to talk to someone after losing Cole. And now that I only had one friend on campus, I desperately needed that connection with someone.

Movement out of the corner of my eye pulled my head to the left. Brooks stepped onto a treadmill two over from mine with his own earbuds in. Of course he did. We couldn't seem to stay out of each other's way.

He didn't look at me as his machine picked up speed, his pace matching mine.

As if he sensed me staring, he looked over. His eyes were emotionless, seemingly bored by my presence. Then just as quickly, he looked away.

Ugh.

I wondered if that would be our thing. Ending up in the same place. Exchanging cold glances. I sent a mental thought up to Cole. 'If this is your idea of karma, I don't like it one bit.' I could imagine him laughing. Wanting to tease me. Saying something about not wanting to leave me with no one to talk football with. I loved talking football. I loved the game. I loved the strategy. And as much as I hated to admit it, Brooks was like Cole. Athletic. Driven. Capable.

Brooks mumbled something I couldn't discern over the volume of my music.

My eyes cut to his. His earbuds dangled over his shoulders. I tugged mine out. "Huh?"

"Just wondering what pearls of wisdom you're gonna bestow upon me today."

"You need to stop hesitating when you drop back," I told him, much to his obvious surprise. "Either do it or don't. Did you see how those guys pummeled you?"

"See it? I was under it."

"Yeah, well, your offensive line sucks. But you can't give the defense a chance to get to you. Know where you're throwing and hit the mark. Your receivers are good. They'll get there."

He stared at me, his eyes narrowed slits.

I wiped my face with the small towel I'd draped over the treadmill screen. "Don't worry, you've got potential."

He choked out a cough. "Potential? I'm the starting quarterback for Alabama."

Those words—especially leaving his mouth—cut deep. The only reason he was playing was because Cole wasn't. He best remember that.

"I've got more than potential," he assured me.

"Yeah," I said, my word clipped as I remembered why I despised him so much. "You've got a massive ego ready to destroy small countries."

"All great athletes have egos. You've got to."

Wow. My hatred toward him was growing by the second. "And you're humble."

He laughed. Didn't he notice I wasn't laughing?

We ran in silence. The pounding of our sneakers on the treadmills mirrored the pounding in my head brought on by his arrogance.

"What's your deal anyway?"

I glanced over at him. "What's that supposed to mean?"

"Not many girls know so much about football *and* wake up at four in the morning to run."

I scoffed. "Hope you're not implying I thought you'd be here."

"I didn't say that."

"But you were thinking it."

He smirked. "You'd be amazed at the lengths girls go to get my attention."

My eyes flared. "I suppose you think I took some crash course in football just to impress you with all my knowledge."

"Just saying."

My face scrunched as I pressed the arrow on the screen to quicken my pace. "Keep dreaming, superstar."

"Girls have done some whacked out shit."

My eyes jumped between the wall in front of me and Brooks. "First of all, I'm not about to steal your towel because it has your sweat on it, nor will I be swiping your jockstrap to sell online. We, my friend, are victims of bad timing."

"Bad timing?"

"Yeah. Anytime you're in my space, it's bad," I assured him as my pace accelerated and my eyes focused on the spot opposite me on the wall.

There was another long silence before Brooks spoke again. "I'm not a good sleeper. It's why I run at four in the morning."

I scoffed. "Well, it seems we have something in common."

"You too?"

I shrugged. "What else is there to do at four in the morning? No one else is up."

He grinned. "Except me."

If I didn't despise him so much, his smile might've stirred something in me. Something that had lain dormant for far too long. "So, you didn't tell me. How do you know so much about football?"

I shrugged. "Grew up around it. Followed Alabama my whole life."

"Now you're living the dream."

"Something like that," I said, knowing better than to bring up Cole.

Though neither of us tucked our earbuds back in, we continued our runs in silence—during which time I counted thirteen marks on the wall, two lights out on my treadmill screen, and two hundred and twenty-seven steps that I'd taken.

"I think we got off on the wrong foot," Brooks said, breaking the silence—and my counting streak.

I glanced over. "I didn't think we were on any foot."

He smiled, not easily put-off by my distaste for him. "I'm Caden."

I tilted my head.

He smirked, well aware I knew who he was. "And you are?"

"Despite what most of your teammates think, I'm not Hey You, Sweetheart, or Water Girl. I'm Finlay."

He pursed his lips as if considering if my name fit. "Well, it's nice to meet you Finlay." He didn't say my name with a southern drawl, the way the local boys said it. It rolled off his tongue smoother. The way a west coaster would say it. "Finlay what?"

My heart drummed faster, and it had nothing to do with the run. It had to do with him being the *last* person I'd open up to about who I was—who my brother was. "Grace." My middle name shot out, technically making it a half-truth and not a total lie. I pressed the button on my machine to slow my pace, needing to cool down before stopping completely.

"I like you," Caden said.

My eyes cut back to his.

"Without the chip on your shoulder."

"I don't have a chip," I growled.

He leveled me with unconvinced eyes, my tone speaking for itself.

"Ever think you just bring out the worst in me?"

He smiled. "Nope. But so you know, we're not all Grady. I, for one, am a pretty decent guy."

"So, the rumors should be ignored?"

"At all costs."

I almost laughed, especially since our conversation was the longest I'd had with anyone, except Sabrina, since arriving to school. And since I'd yet to leave his sorry ass alone in the gym, I'd apparently been starved for conversation of any sort.

"What the hell is this?" Coach's voice echoed through the room, yanking our attention to him standing in the doorway with fiery eyes.

"Morning Coach," Caden greeted him with a grin, like we hadn't just broken a team rule.

Coach's eyes shot to mine. "I expected this from Brooks, Finlay. But not you."

My eyes cast down as I switched off my treadmill. I never wanted to do anything to upset the man who gave me a chance to start over and heal. "I'm sorry, Coach. I probably should've warned you. I have trouble sleeping."

"Oh, I…" Coach's voice trailed off uncomfortably.

I jumped off my treadmill as it came to a stop.

The regret in his eyes spoke volumes. "Well next time just text me. Let me know you've left your room."

I nodded.

"And you." He glared at Caden, his finger pointing at him as his treadmill slowed to a stop. "You know better." He gave Caden no time to respond, turning and walking out of the gym without another word.

Once silence descended, Caden looked to me. "*I* know better but next time just text him? Seriously?"

I shrugged, knowing better than to elaborate. "Must be the girl thing."

"What girl thing?"

"You know, the way guys get all uncomfortable when girls mention their periods. Insomnia must have the same effect on him."

Caden shook his head. "I have no problem with it."

"Bullshit."

He stepped off his treadmill. "I swear. I've bought tampons before."

"I don't believe you," I said.

"You know there's no way I can prove it."

I hitched my thumb toward the doorway. "There's a gift shop right off the lobby."

He laughed, and when he laughed like that I almost forgot I hated him.

* * *

I could barely see out of my bloodshot eyes. A revolving door of unfamiliar faces passed by me, shaking my hand and uttering their apologies. Each offering heartfelt words that were supposed to console me, but all they really did was just jumble together into a cacophony of noise in my silent head. I was dazed, but doing better than my mother who couldn't even stand without her knees buckling. My father did most of the talking. I just nodded and said my thanks. Really, what more was there for me to say? My brother was gone and my life as I knew it was over.

"Finlay. Can I get you anything?"

My eyes lifted to Hazel, our old neighbor, who had stepped into the line to check on me, her face filled with sadness.

I shook my head.

Her eyes swept over the room. "Look at all the people who came out to pay their respects."

My eyes shifted, moving around the crowded room. Every seat was filled with family members, neighbors, and classmates. A line of people wrapped around the room, currently biding their time before they moved to the front of the line. It was sad really. They waited to get to the front to kneel at a casket that held my dead brother before facing my mom, dad, and me. To say what? Cole was a great guy? He didn't deserve to die so young?

I just wanted the day to be over. No, I needed it to be over. I needed it to have all just been a bad dream. I wanted to mourn alone. I wanted to have time to myself to dwell on my regret. My guilt. My selfishness. But everyone was making it so damn difficult.

"Did you see his football team came? There's a big bus outside," Hazel continued.

My eyes strayed to the large bodies in line, waiting patiently for Hazel to move away so they could pay their respects. Had they even really gotten to know Cole? I knew he was their starting quarterback, the first freshman to get the role in years, but the season hadn't even begun. Had he made new friends I didn't know about? Had he hung out with these guys? Had he told them about his bitch of a sister?

Each player moved by me, shaking my hand. Most didn't even make eye contact. Did I look that bad? The tight bun meant to hide my failed attempt at going blond did little to disguise my swollen eyes and blotchy cheeks stained with tears. But for his teammates to look away all together, it must have been a combination of my devastation and their own discomfort.

"Sorry," a massive guy said as he moved by me, eyes on his shoes.

"Cole was a great guy," another uttered softly looking at the guy's back in front of him.

"I'm sorry," another said until his words just blended in with all the others who followed.

By the time they'd all passed, Coach Burns approached me. He'd visited our house several times last year to entice Cole to Alabama, promising future glories with him at the helm. He'd also been the one to rush to our home after the police officers delivered the news. In line, he wrapped his arms around me and whispered. "I'm so sorry this happened, Finlay. I'm so sorry it happened on my watch."

Hearing his guilt brought on a whole new bout of tears.

He pulled back with regret etched deeply in every wrinkle around his eyes.

"Thanks, Coach."

He moved on to my mother, bending down to her seated in the chair beside me. He wrapped her in the same tight hug and she clutched onto him as if he were her last direct line to Cole. I couldn't hear what he uttered to her as my hand was already shaking the next person's, but it caused my mother to weep. I looked away, knowing her tears brought on my tears. I needed to stay strong. I needed to be strong.

My eyes latched onto movement outside the window. The football players made their way solemnly back to the bus in a single file. They'd only known Cole for such a short time. They couldn't possibly understand the devastation I felt. They couldn't possibly know what an amazing guy and athlete they'd lost.

Lost. As if he just wandered off somewhere. Somewhere I'd be able to find him. Just like when we were kids playing hide-and-seek.

Before I could tear my eyes away, one of the guys patted another on the shoulder. The player who received the pat turned around with a giant smile on his face. But he wasn't just smiling, he was laughing as he lifted his fist and bumped knuckles with his teammate. Why was he laughing and celebrating as he left a funeral home? A funeral home where his dead teammate remained. Wasn't he sad? Wasn't he just as angry that this happened as I was?

His insensitivity felt like a dagger to my chest. How could he actually be happy at a moment like this? How could he feel joy when my whole world had just been ripped away from me?

That night I couldn't shake his callousness. Couldn't shake my anger. Couldn't shake my disgust. I pulled up the Alabama team roster on my phone, looking for the guy behind the laughter. Behind the fist-bump.

Caden Brooks.

Second string quarterback.

My heart sank and my stomach roiled. No wonder he was so happy. He'd be getting Cole's position. He'd be getting to live Cole's dream. And he was happy about it. Happy my brother was gone.

That was the moment. The moment I swore to hate Caden Brooks with everything I had.

CHAPTER SEVEN

Finlay

I stared at my dorm room ceiling as I lay on my bed. I should've been studying. I should've been writing an essay. I should've been calling to check on my parents. But all I could do was stare at the glow-in-the-dark stars above my bed. Some days were definitely easier than others. And today, one of very few days I had off, I didn't know how to handle not having to rush from class to class then the field for practice. My life was a non-stop loop, one that left little time to dwell on anything but school and football.

"Guess what?"

My eyes shifted to Sabrina walking through the door. "I'm getting my big sister next week."

"Big sister? I thought you're an only child?"

She laughed as she closed the door and dropped down beside me on my bed. "No. In the sorority. You get a big sister. You know, to help you through pledging."

"O-kay."

She laughed. "It's just a fun thing they do."

"Got it." Sounded lame to me. But since she was loving the whole pledging thing, who was I to criticize it?

"I've been trying to figure out who might pick me. You know, who's been paying extra attention to me. But I just can't figure it out."

"Well, look at it this way. It'll be a big surprise."

"*Big*. Look at you. Nice one."

I laughed. I wasn't used to joking around with other girls. Even growing up, I got along better with boys. They weren't into drama and they enjoyed sports like me. But maybe things were changing now that I'd left home. Maybe I was actually starting to let people in again.

"What do you say we do nothing for the rest of the day but pig out on junk food while binge watching some old show neither of us has seen on Netflix?"

I could see how hard she was trying to include me and get close to me. I appreciated it. It had been a long time since someone cared about what I was doing. Sure, my parents cared. But they had their own grief to contend with. I guess it was about time for me to start living again. "I'd like that."

"See. I told you pledging wouldn't take me away from my favorite roommate."

"I'm your only roommate."

"And a great one at that," she said with a smile.

"You have to say that."

"Oh, honey. This southern girl says nothing she doesn't mean."

* * *

I was already well into my book as the team began boarding the bus for our trip to Louisiana that Friday. Yvette analyzed whatever it was she analyzed for Coach

Burns in the window seat beside me. I glanced up just as Caden made his way down the aisle. He stopped beside me and dropped a plastic bag into my lap. "Here," he said with a smirk, before moving down the aisle.

Not wanting to appear too eager, I sat for a long time staring at the bag in my lap. When I couldn't take the suspense any longer, I opened the bag. That son-of-a-bitch. He bought me a box of tampons.

"Well, that was weird," Yvette said, subtly peeking inside the bag.

I laughed, both surprised by her reaction and amused by Caden's nerve—and the fact that he waited almost a week to pull it off. "It was kind of a bet."

She nodded before returning to her charts.

I glanced over my shoulder, instantly locking eyes with Caden. He lifted an eyebrow, a victory dance no doubt. I shook my head before turning back to the front and tucking the bag into my backpack with thoughts of payback on my mind.

* * *

No matter what Caden did, Louisiana's defense put pressure on him to get rid of the ball. His offensive line looked terrible which made him look terrible and caused the team to record their first loss.

When I rolled my cart into the locker room after the game, I knew not to make eye contact with anyone. They were pissed and so was Coach.

"What the fuck Grady?" Caden yelled as he stormed into the locker room, slamming his helmet down on the ground.

"You're gonna wanna keep yourself away from me," Grady warned as Caden cornered him, backing him into a wall. Grady easily had a hundred pounds on him. And in a fight, Grady would win. But to see Caden so fired up and ready to throw down, he'd clearly had enough.

"You threw me to the fucking wolves out there," Caden said, not backing down.

Grady cocked his head, like Caden's claim held no weight.

That was it. Caden lunged forward and shoved him, causing Grady to stumble back into the wall. "You're supposed to be the best. Isn't that what you tell everyone?"

Grady's eyes dropped to where Caden shoved his chest. His head shot up. The anger he should've shown on the field reared its ugly head. He lunged faster than I'd ever seen him move and he hauled off on Caden's face. But Caden didn't back down. Even with blood dripping from his nose, he went after Grady, wailing on his face.

It was a train wreck I just couldn't pull my eyes away from.

Players jumped in, grabbing them and pulling them off each other. Neither Grady nor Caden stopped throwing punches even as they were yanked apart. "You son of a bitch!" Grady yelled.

"You don't deserve your position," Caden yelled back. "A cheerleader could do better!"

"I fucking hate you," Grady growled, breathless and out for Caden's blood.

"Feeling's mutual, asshole," Caden yelled, his arms determined to grab Grady.

"That's enough!" Coach Burns' voice cut through the melee.

Everyone froze.

"Both of you. In the office now." Coach stormed off, leaving them to straighten themselves out and follow him into the office with their proverbial tails between their legs.

* * *

I tossed the hotel towel onto a poolside chair and dove into the indoor pool in my black bikini. Being four in the morning, it was dark, quiet, and I didn't have to worry about anyone else being there.

I broke through the water's surface and pulled in a breath. The pungent smell of chlorine cleared my senses. I dropped my head back into the water and lifted my legs, moving my arms in circles beneath the water to steer as I floated on my back. Underwater, silence surrounded me. I could've taken a shower to rid my body of the sweat I woke up in, but coach's understanding that sometimes I needed to do what I needed to do, motivated me to take a swim.

I floated for a long time, letting nothing but solace envelop me. Not regret. Not guilt. Not sadness.

Last night's nationally televised game had been a close one. And even though Caden was more focused, taking his time with his throws, Grady and his line couldn't get their act together. I wondered what Coach said to them behind closed doors because when they boarded the bus to head back to the hotel sometime after eleven, neither of them looked happy.

I slipped underwater, swimming until I reached the side of the pool. I surfaced and pushed my hair back out of my face before grasping the cement around the pool.

"Don't let me stop you," Caden's deep voice echoed through the room.

My body tensed as I struggled to find him in the dark room. His shadow grew as he stood from a chair and walked to the edge of the pool, stopping at my fingertips. My eyes drifted from his bare feet up to his solid calves over his cargo shorts until they stopped on his bare chest. *Holy hell.* Why wasn't he wearing a shirt? "Are you coming in?"

"Do you want me to?" His voice was low and raspy, something I'd never heard out of his mouth before—especially directed at me.

"Not really."

He snickered at the apparent fear in my voice. "You weren't in the gym."

"Were you trying to bring me more tampons?"

He shook his head, the smirk on his face undeniable. "I think I made my point."

"And what was that?"

"I'm always up for a challenge."

"Is that so?"

He nodded. "And I was a little curious where you were."

"Well, not to worry. Running isn't my only talent. I'm a good swimmer, too."

He hitched his thumb over his shoulder. "From where I was sitting, you're a good floater."

My head shot back. "How long have you been in here?"

He shrugged. "Long enough *not* to see you swim."

I laughed. "You sure your eyes aren't playing tricks on you? That's quite a shiner you've got."

He stifled a smile. "Have you seen Grady's face?"

"You guys kiss and make up?"

"Kiss Grady? No. Come to an understanding? Maybe. But with him, what he hears and does are two completely different things." He shook his head. "The guy's such a douche."

"Can't argue with that." I reached my hand out to him. "Mind giving me a hand?"

He reached down and grabbed my hand. His dry grip was strong—quite a contrast to my cold pruned fingers. He could've pulled my entire body out with one tug. But that wasn't what I wanted. Instead I tugged his hand hard, throwing him off balance. He tried catching himself, but fell into the water with a huge splash.

I scrambled back, not wanting to be anywhere near him when he surfaced.

When he did, his eyes were wild, searching the pool for me. I assumed his eyes had adjusted to the darkness because he spotted me on the low end, a sly smile swiping across his face. "You thought that was funny?" He pushed his hair off his forehead.

I nodded as I stifled my laughter. "As funny as a box of tampons in my lap."

"So that's how it's gonna be?" He moved toward me, wiping water from his eyes as he did. "An eye for an eye?"

"Just following your lead." I kept him in my sight as I moved along the wall, lowering my body so only my head remained above water.

"Then why are you all the way over there?" He moved closer, treading water easily as I shuffled away from him. "You wanted me in the water. Here I am."

My pulse began to rattle in my chest. "I didn't think you'd actually fall in."

He grunted incredulously. "You pulled my hand, but didn't think I'd fall in?"

I shook my head. "I wanted to scare you."

"Do I look scared?" His eyes tightened, predatory and sexy as hell. If I was capable of falling under his spell, I very well could have in that moment. But his charms were wasted on me. He lunged forward until he had me backed into the curved corner of the pool.

I moved right. He was there. I tried for left. He was there, too. *Shit.*

"Now, what to do with you," he mused.

Thankfully we were cloaked in darkness because heat crept up my neck, spreading to my cheeks. "I'm sorry."

He raised a brow. "Now you're sorry?"

I nodded, unsure what he was looking for.

His features remained pensive as he tunneled his fingers through his wet hair, his biceps all shiny and ripped.

Oh, man. I needed to remember why I hated him so much. I needed to get away from him. Far away. I dropped underwater and pushed off the wall behind me, taking off swimming. I didn't get far. Caden wrapped his arms around my waist, pulling me against his chest.

I froze.

It took all of two seconds of having his wet skin and rock hard body wrapped around me for the image of him dropping his lips to my bare shoulder to materialize in my brain. A shiver surged through me. In that instant, when being in his arms felt too good, I knew I needed to get out of there. I wiggled my body, fighting to break loose from his grasp.

"Woah. Relax." He released my waist, but grabbed hold of my shoulders and spun me toward him. "I'm not used to girls fighting to get away from me."

Being that close to him caused my eyes to cast down, a desperate attempt to reel in my hormones—and sanity.

"Hey." He lifted my chin with his finger. All I could do was stare at the clumped lashes surrounding his black eye. "I was just teasing you. I wouldn't hurt you."

I nodded. "I know."

"So what is it? You don't like guys touching you or something?"

I swallowed around a lump, realizing how easy it would've been for him to lean in and kiss me in that dark pool with no one else around. But it would've been just as easy to deliver him a second black eye. And given his gaze now focused on my lips, he needed a reminder. "I don't like guys with girlfriends touching me."

His hands vanished from my shoulders so quickly you'd think he'd been zapped by a large dose of electricity. Or in this case, reality. "Yeah. Sorry about that."

I shrugged. "I just prefer the single kind. Unless of course it's Grady. Then I just want to kick him in the balls."

Caden laughed a low raspy laugh, the kind that reached all the way down to my core. It was intoxicating. And wrong on so many levels. He moved back. "I really am sorry." His words held little conviction.

Yet the truth remained. He had a girlfriend. And despite the way he'd been pushing his way into my life, I needed to hate him. If not for me, for Cole.

CHAPTER EIGHT

Finlay

"What's that?" Sabrina stepped through the door of our room Sunday night. Her bathrobe was knotted tightly around her waist and her wet hair sat in a sloppy knot on the top of her head.

I fumbled with the Alabama jersey I held, quickly rolling it into a ball and tucking it into my side so I practically sat on it. "Oh, nothing."

She closed the door behind her. "Does *nothing* have to do with one of those fine football players you spend all your time with?"

I cocked my head. "If you only knew what they were really like, you wouldn't be so intrigued by them."

She placed her shower caddy on the floor of her closet. "Intrigued?" She turned back around. "Honey, I'm not intrigued. I'm jealous as hell."

Our laughter filled the room. I loved having her around to talk to. I may not have been ready to open up to her about everything, but I appreciated her giving me space and letting me open up gradually. When I told her that Cole died, she apologized for bringing him up and told me how sorry she was, never bringing him up again. It was weird. Sometimes I appreciated people steering clear of the subject so it didn't send me into a tailspin. Other times I felt guilty for not talking about him more. Cole existed. He played a huge role in my life. He was an amazing brother and should be remembered and talked about.

So why was it so damn hard?

"So, tell me." Sabrina dropped onto her bed. "All those long bus rides and nights in hotel rooms. You can't tell me you haven't been propositioned—or at least felt up."

I choked on a laugh, knowing what happened in the pool needed to remain in that pool. "First of all, if any of them touched me, they'd have a knee to their junk."

She snorted.

"And second, they're not interested in me." My eyes swept down at my worn T-shirt with the hole under the arm and my long shorts. "I'm not what you call, their type."

"Finlay, you're hot. I'm not sure why you insist on covering your curves with clothes that don't flaunt that bod, or why you never do anything with that hair but pull it back into a ponytail. But don't fool yourself. Guys are guys. And I'm guessing, most of them are envisioning what's *really* under there."

I rolled my eyes, appreciating her trying to boost my self-esteem.

"I've seen the pictures on your board. You were adorable. And that homecoming picture. Girl, you looked hot."

I sighed. "That was a long time ago."

"Before Cole died?" she asked tentatively.

I nodded. "After losing him, everything just lost its meaning. Things I thought were important, weren't anymore. Besides, it's not like I've got anyone to impress."

She tilted her head thoughtfully. "But you're in college now. It's time for a fresh start. No one knows you. It's a chance to be whoever you want to be."

Monday morning, I pulled some clothes I hadn't unpacked from a box in my closet. I slipped on a pair of torn cutoffs and a sleeveless black shirt with horizontal slits in the back. I left my hair down, doing nothing to the waves but tossing them over my shoulder and heading out. Sabrina had been right. Starting over didn't require concealing every part of me. Hell, I was still a twenty-year-old girl with a pretty good body. What was the use in hiding it?

Inside the lecture hall, I took my seat in the back of the middle section. Grady must've been too wiped out from the weekend travel since he wasn't there. My eyes flashed toward the entrance. But it wasn't Grady who walked in. It was Caden, all his innate confidence there for the room to see. His eyes scanned the seats, particularly the seats around me. A small smile slid across his face once he spotted me. My eyes dropped to my laptop perched on my lap. We weren't friends. We weren't anything.

The professor began his lecture a few minutes later. My eyes lifted. I couldn't help the fact that they drifted to where Caden sat…right beside his girlfriend. Her hand was wrapped around the back of his neck, playing with his hair. What would she have thought if she knew he'd had his hands on *me* in the pool?

Caden

What the hell was Finlay wearing? Even from half a lecture hall away I could see those long legs resting on the back of the chair in front of her. Sure, I could *feel* her hot little body when I grabbed her in the pool. But it had been dark. Now in broad daylight, or at least the daylight streaming through the skylights in the lecture hall, I could see her damn legs went on for miles.

What was it about her that toyed with my head? Intrigued me? Maybe it was the fact that she challenged me. That she liked football and actually knew the game. I'm not saying I wanted in her pants, I just knew I liked being around her even though she clearly hated being around me.

Leslie scratched the spot on the back of my head that she knew drove me wild. Could she sense my attention was elsewhere? I leaned over and nuzzled her neck, letting her know all was good. When I sat upright, I caught her small smile as her hand slipped away. I was good at reading girls. Every girl but Finlay. Why the hell was she always so hot and cold with me?

I glanced over my shoulder, stretching out my sore neck. Saturday night's game had been brutal. My offensive line allowed too many through, getting me sacked and forced to intentionally ground. Neither was acceptable. But regardless of the poor coverage, I did what Finlay suggested and didn't hesitate. I set my feet and hit my targets. It definitely kept me from getting pummeled more times than I should've—thanks to fucking Grady.

I looked to his usual seat. It was empty. He clearly hadn't dragged his lazy ass out of bed. And he wasn't bothering Finlay who typed away at her laptop. She was cute when she was focused. Damn cute. Was that why she always covered up and sported that stoic face? Did she want to keep the guys on the team at bay?

She was certainly different. Most girls would've loved the fact that I had my arms around them. But not her. She couldn't get away quickly enough. And she still insisted on putting me in my place by bringing up Leslie. Leslie, who'd rearranged her schedule to take two classes with me and wanted nothing more than to help me.

Was I really going to spend my time thinking about a girl who wasn't Leslie? One who couldn't stand me fifty percent of the time? One who was nothing like the sort of girl I usually went for? Hell, no. I had football and school I needed to focus on.

After class, Leslie and I grabbed breakfast in the commuter café in the student union. She always sat next to me. It usually didn't bother me, but today it did. I felt like I couldn't breathe with her up in my space. I felt like she wanted everyone in that room to know I was off limits. But despite what she believed, I belonged to no one. No one but me.

"What's wrong?"

My eyes cut to hers. "Huh?"

She shrugged. "I don't know. You're just off. Ever since you got back."

I bit into my bagel sandwich and spoke with my mouth full. "No idea."

She sat for a long time quietly sipping her latte, like she thought I'd eventually tell her if she waited long enough. When I didn't, she spoke. "Did I tell you about the house my daddy found on the coast?"

I shrugged. Her father was a luxury real estate agent and his job had become a hot topic of conversation for her lately.

"Well, it's a cute ten-bedroom home that overlooks the water." She grabbed her phone from the table and tapped away at the screen.

"Ten bedrooms?" I said between bites. "Who needs that many rooms?"

She grinned. "Us."

That was the sucker-punch to the gut I hadn't been expecting. It might've been my longest relationship to date, but not if she kept that shit up. "Us?"

She placed her hand on my forearm, rubbing it for what I could only imagine came next. "Yes, us. I always plan for the future."

I nearly choked on my next bite. "And that future entails a ten-bedroom house?"

She held up her phone, showing me the ginormous house on the screen. "Give or take a few rooms."

What. The. Fuck? My food felt like rocks going down my throat. Had she gone and lost her fucking mind while I was away? The future to me was my next game. Nothing after that. And apparently, she needed to understand that before she started choosing furniture to fill that obnoxious house. "Let me just focus on the season and see where that takes me."

Hurt replaced her eager, future-planning eyes. "Oh, yeah. Of course."

I turned my head, not wanting to see her disappointment. I didn't want to hurt her, but come the fuck on. I was a twenty-one-year-old guy with professional football aspirations. I may have been committed at the moment, but that moment was seriously coming to an end if she didn't back off with all the future talk.

The room had filled up around us. People breezed through for a quick bite while others settled in with notebooks and laptops, meeting others to study.

I had a feeling Leslie's push for the future had something to do with the rumors spreading across campus that I planned to declare myself eligible for the draft at the end of the season. The crazy thing was I hadn't even made up my mind yet. Sure, I wanted to go pro eventually, but skipping senior year altogether was a big decision. And not once had Leslie asked me about it. She just believed the rumors. Believed she had reason to start planning for the future.

"You haven't mentioned New Orleans. How was it?" she asked, pulling me from my thoughts.

"Did you watch the game?"

She nodded. "I went home for the weekend. Daddy had all his friends over. You looked great out there."

"What game were you watching?"

Her phone pinged with a text. "Well, you looked hot in your uniform."

"Leslie, we lost. My line clearly sucks which makes me suck."

She didn't look at me as her thumbs flew across her screen. "They do?"

I nodded vehemently. "I'm shocked I made any completions at all. I'm working on getting rid of the ball faster when I drop back."

"Drop what?"

"Drop back."

She looked up from her phone, an unfathomable expression on her face.

"Never mind." My eyes drifted back to the crowded room. I would've been lying if I said I wasn't looking for someone in particular. Someone who understood all the ins and outs of the game. Someone who was becoming increasingly more relevant in my world.

Dammit.

* * *

By the time I reached the practice field, I was already exhausted. From traveling to Louisiana over the weekend to catching up on school work and cramming in game films, I'd forgotten how tired I felt once football season was in full swing. But I wouldn't trade it for anything in the world. I loved it. I loved every fucking minute of it.

"Brooks!" Coach shouted as I reached the sideline, my helmet in hand and my practice gear on.

"What's up, Coach?"

"You watch the films?"

I nodded as I stepped up beside him.

"What'd you think of Arkansas' defense?"

"They're out for blood." I could still hear the crunch of Sanders' bones when they hit him from both sides.

"And then some," he agreed. "We've got to work with the line on amping up protection. The boys have what it takes, but you're not a unit out there. I know it and you know it. It's like you all have your own agendas. And after yours and Grady's locker room display, everyone knows it."

I nodded. Playing on the same team didn't make us friends. After practice and games, we went our separate ways. But I knew what the coach was saying. If we wanted to win, we needed to mesh on and off the field. My offensive line didn't have an intrinsic need to protect me. But after our first two games, how could I trust these guys when they were missing easy tackles that led to me getting crushed?

"On the field *I* can handle it." Coach said. "Off the field, I need *you* to figure it out. If you don't, you better expect hits from Arkansas' defense on Saturday."

"Got it, Coach."

He walked away, leaving me to figure out what the hell I was going to do. There was no way I wanted to hang out with guys like Grady off the field. The guy was a complete douchebag. But if we could jive off the field, that could translate onto the field and save my life and my professional prospects.

I glanced onto the field where Grady and the rest of the offensive line worked with the line coach. They needed some motivation if they were gonna have my back. They needed to *want* to protect me at all costs. I spotted Finlay standing near a table lining up her water bottles like a champ. "Hey."

She glanced over her shoulder, lifting her chin in my direction. We hadn't spoken since I decided to feel her up in the pool. She probably hated me. I guess I couldn't blame her. It was a dick move.

"Can I ask a favor?"

She shrugged, her wavy dark hair bouncing over her shoulders. It looked pretty down like that. Even more so up close than in the lecture hall.

"Can I borrow your phone?"

She cocked her head. "If this is some lame attempt to get your number in my phone, I'm not interested."

I knew she was kidding around by the facetious glint in her eye, but the truth remained. There was something about me that rubbed her the wrong way. Something that made her want nothing to do with me. I held out my hand, not bothering with a response.

She pulled her phone from the back pocket of her cutoffs. Cutoffs that displayed those insanely long legs again. Sweet Jesus. I needed to get my head in check. Both of them.

I took the phone and punched in Leslie's number. "Hey," I said as soon as Leslie answered.

"Whose number is this?" she asked.

"Finlay's. I—"

"Who's Finlay?" I could hear the irritation in her voice.

"The water girl." I glanced to Finlay who swiftly spun away from me. *Shit.* I forgot she hated when the guys referred to her that way.

"Why are you using the water girl's phone?" Leslie persisted.

"To call you," I huffed, irritated with her inquisition and possessiveness. "Listen. Coach wants me to put together a team bonding thing with some of the guys. You think you can rally your sisters tonight?"

There was silence on her end.

"Leslie?"

"I'm here. I'm just wondering if you even realize you're asking me to pimp out my sisters."

"Pimp out your sisters?"

"Yes."

I considered it. "Maybe just a little."

"You're an asshole."

"I just need them to hang out with my offensive line and have a little fun—if they can manage to take the sticks out of their asses for a little while."

"Caden. That's not fair. You know we have a certain reputation to uphold."

"Oh my God, Leslie. You sound like a sorority handbook."

She huffed. Nothing about it made me believe she wouldn't come through.

"So, you in?"

She sighed. "I'll bring them by after our pledge event."

"Great. See you tonight." I disconnected the call and held the phone out to Finlay. "Thanks."

Finlay turned around with her hand extended. She couldn't despise me as much as she wanted me to think she did. I placed the phone in her hand, purposely grazing my fingertips over her palm. As expected, she yanked her hand away and tucked her phone into her shorts.

"Coach is on my ass to bring the guys together," I explained.

She nodded. "I don't blame him. You guys aren't working well out there."

She'd seen our interactions. It was tough keeping up appearances in front of the staff. "It's easier said than done when you're dealing with idiots like Grady."

She shrugged, almost sympathetically. "Sounds like you're trying. But wouldn't strippers be better? A bunch of stuck-up sorority girls doesn't scream fun to me."

"Then you've never seen drunk sorority girls." I laughed, having seen my fair share.

"Yeah. It's totally not my scene."

I believed that. "Well, thanks for the phone."

"Don't thank me now. I plan on calling your girlfriend at three in the morning when I know you're with her, just for fun."

I laughed, but something about the way she said it told me I should probably expect a call at three in the morning.

CHAPTER NINE

Finlay

"Whose house is this?" I asked Sabrina as we made our way up the front porch of a house on the outskirts of campus. Given the loud music blaring from the open windows aglow with lights, the two-story house attracted more than its fair share of attention.

"More chicks," a loud voice announced as the screen door scraped open.

My eyes met the cold eyes of my nemesis as he stepped out onto the porch with a ruthless smile across his face. "Never mind. It's just the water girl," Grady said. "You gonna be my beer bitch tonight, too, water girl?"

Sabrina eyed me wearily as we made our way up the steps.

"Dealing with assholes like him is just one of the perks of my job," I said casually to Sabrina, before leveling Grady with a glare. "You gonna move so we can come in or what?" My bravado lasted all of two seconds when a cold shudder scrambled up my spine. If

Grady was here, when he should have been at his team bonding night, then—

Dammit.

"By all means." Grady swept out his arm like he was a gentleman. His gaze slid to Sabrina as he swiftly morphed into another person all together. "And who do we have here?"

She smiled, dazzling him with her beyond-white smile. "The beer bitch's roommate. And if you even think about looking at us in there, I'll replace your beer with pee. Now move."

The dude had the ability to crush opponents for breakfast—when he wasn't being such a screw-up—but my hundred-pound roommate brought him to his knees. He stepped out of our way.

"That was awesome," I whispered over the music as we crossed the threshold and were out of Grady's earshot.

She shrugged. "The guy's a douche."

I laughed, but the truth remained. I shouldn't have been there. "Maybe I should just go."

"Are you kidding? You can't leave me here," she hissed back. "This is one of the first events I've been invited to by the sisters. I can't not show."

I followed her down the hallway, glancing into the rooms. Football players and sorority girls with red cups milled around the scarce mismatched furniture. Apparently the athletic code of conduct's No Alcohol policy was null and void when it came to team bonding. A few of the guys from the team lifted their cups in my direction. Feeling completely out of place, I smiled back as I followed Sabrina to the kitchen. People filled the small space, most surrounding the keg in a big bucket beside the refrigerator. I kept my eyes down, not wanting to run into—

"Finlay?"

Shit. I slowly lifted my gaze in the direction of his voice.

Caden moved toward me with a cup in his hand. "What are you doing here?"

His question tightened a knot in my stomach. He clearly didn't want me there. Who could blame him? One minute I'm joking around with him, the next I hate him. I can barely tolerate myself when he's around. "I can leave if—"

"No. That's not what I meant. I just didn't think this was your scene."

I shrugged. "My roommate's pledging a sorority. She was invited. I guess you're pimping her out, too."

He laughed, his eyes flashing away in embarrassment. "You heard that part, huh?"

I nodded. "The word pimp in any conversation perks up the ears."

"I'll have to remember that," he said before sipping his drink.

We stood awkwardly for a minute. I glanced around at the girls on one side of the room and the guys on the other. It looked more like an eighth-grade dance than what I envisioned a college party to be like. "So, are you waiting for them to get drunk or do you have another plan to start the bonding?"

He shrugged. "Usually it's just a free-for-all, especially with Forester here."

"He's your roommate?"

He nodded. "He had plans tonight which was good because I only invited the offensive line. Figured if he and the rest of the guys were here, there'd still be that divide." His eyes swept the room. "But I don't really know these guys off the field."

I glanced around the lifeless room, a definite contrast to the upbeat music blaring. It was gonna take a miracle to get these guys on the same page. "Get me a stack of cups," I said to Caden.

"Huh?"

"Cups. I need a stack."

His apprehension told me he didn't trust me. But he turned to the counter and grabbed a sleeve of red cups, handing them to me.

I knew what was on the line if Caden didn't deliver. The guys would continue to fight, remaining strangers on and off the field. And that would never work. The more we lost, the angrier everyone would get. And working for angry guys was no walk in the park. Besides, I was still an Alabama fan at heart. And my team needed to win.

I walked over to the kitchen table where four linemen squeezed into the chairs around it, emphasizing their massive sizes more so than on the field.

"Hey, water girl," Lemer said as I stepped in front of them.

"Didn't even recognize you with your hair down," Miller added, the sleeves of tattoos wrapped around his massive biceps intimidating if you didn't know what a softy he was.

I smiled. "You guys up for a game of flip cup?"

"Hell yeah," Lemer said, as the others joined him, pushing back their chairs and standing, two on each side of the table.

After lining the table with four cups on each side, I hurried to the keg and filled a cup which I used to fill each cup on the table with a couple inches of beer. I scanned the room for girls to play with them. I approached a few standing in the corner by the refrigerator. "Anyone wanna play flip cup?"

Two of the girls walked to the table, introducing themselves and joining a team. The guys' smiles were almost comical. But even with the girls, both teams still needed another player. I hurried down the hallway to find Sabrina who'd disappeared as soon as we got inside.

A hand on my upper arm stopped me mid-step. I knew the hand. I'd felt it on my wet skin. And it wasn't any less daunting in a house full of people. I steeled myself and looked over my shoulder.

"Where are you going?" Caden asked.

"They need two more players."

He shook his head. "I've got two."

My eyes shot around. "Yeah?"

He nodded, amusement dancing in his eyes. "You and me."

"I don't think so."

"Scared?"

My head recoiled. "Of what?"

He snickered. "Oh, I don't know. Actually having fun? Letting loose?"

"I have fun." Nothing about what I said sounded convincing.

He cocked his head.

That just pissed me off. "Maybe I don't like the company," I said, fixing my chin in place.

He scoffed. "Yeah, you keep saying that. But then we keep ending up in the same place."

I opened my mouth to respond.

"Brooks, you playing?" Miller shouted.

"Yup." Caden said, staring at me with a giant grin. "So is Finlay,"

"Who's Finlay?" Jacobs, another teammate, asked.

I raised my hand as I walked over to a vacant spot behind the cup at the end of the table. "Everyone's favorite water girl."

Caden took the spot across from me staring me down with a satisfied smirk.

The game started and the beer began flowing like water. Puddles were all over the table and floor. A couple times I nearly slipped as I worked to flip my cup before the other team. That just made me laugh louder than I already was. I had no idea what had gotten into me—besides a shitload of beer. But I wasn't alone. Everyone else at the table was laughing and cheering just as loudly as they struggled to flip their cups right side up. Half the party, including Grady and Sabrina, had circled the table to watch and cheer along with us.

"Water girl's got this," Miller chanted as I tossed down the beer then flipped my cup which kept falling on its side.

"Shit," I screeched. The harder I tried to flip it, the worse it got. It always came down to Caden and me, the two at the end of the table. I could see him across from me having just as much trouble.

"Not this time, Finlay," Caden warned as he flipped his cup unsuccessfully. "I've got this."

"Watch and learn, Brooks," I laughed. "I've got skills you've never seen before."

"I don't doubt it," he said in an undertone. One I wasn't even sure I'd heard in my quest to flip my cup faster than him.

But I wouldn't be distracted. I focused every bit of energy I had on flipping my stupid cup. My team cheered me on as my cup, after several failed attempts, finally landed right side up. I threw my hands up in the air. Miller, who played beside me, swept me up in his massive arms and spun me around. I laughed, but it did nothing for my head, already on the verge of spinning from so much alcohol. I glanced to Caden who continued to fumble with his cup across the table as everyone around us laughed and shouted.

"Put her down, Miller," Caden said, finally giving up on his cup that lay on its side.

The room stopped spinning as Miller placed me back down on my feet. I grasped the wet surface of the table to regain my balance. "Thanks," I mouthed to Caden.

He shrugged, and for some reason, I couldn't seem to tear my eyes from him. It was as if every sound and every person in that room had disappeared as I absorbed the details of his face. His blue eyes were so pretty, and they were still staring at me. I normally avoided his expressive eyes, worried what time spent with him would do to my head. But with liquor flowing freely through my veins, I just wanted to look for a little while longer. His eyes narrowed, and I wondered what he was thinking as he stared back at me. My breathing became shallow as I struggled to remember why I hated him so much. I tried with everything I had to conjure that image two years ago. His smile. His fist bump. His blatant disregard for my suffering. But it had become foggy, fleeting with each passing moment. My heartbeat sped as I fought to hold onto the image, but all I could think about was his hands on me in the pool.

"Caden," a female's voice broke through my drunken mind's ramblings, yanking my eyes away from him. Caden's girlfriend stood in the doorway with her arms crossed, her eyes staring him down like a parent who'd caught her teenager throwing a raging party.

Without hesitation, Caden stalked toward her, grabbed her cheeks and pulled her mouth to his.

My stomach churned as he shoved his tongue down her throat for the room to see. "I'll be right back," I told my teammates as I took off unsteadily down the hallway to the bathroom. Luckily, I didn't have to wait in line. I closed the door behind me and dropped down on the toilet with my pants still in place. I buried my face in my palms, trying to steady my labored breaths and pounding heart.

Why the hell had I been enjoying myself? Why was seeing Caden kissing his *girlfriend* an unwelcome sight? Why was I there in the first place?

A knock on the door pulled me from my thoughts. "Hold on," I called, shaking my head and clearing away the uncertainty. I stood and braced my hands on the bathroom sink, staring into the mirror above it. My cheeks were flushed and, despite the sweat I'd felt while racing to win the stupid drinking game, my hair actually looked nice. I wondered if Caden noticed.

Oh, hell no.

I needed to get out of there. And I needed to get out of there fast. It was no place for a drunk me. I tore out of the bathroom with one mission in mind. Finding Sabrina. I found her, ironically enough, sitting with Caden's girlfriend on the living room sofa.

Her eyes lifted to mine, a hopeful smile spreading across her face. "Finlay. You did great in there. It looked like you were having fun."

My eyes jumped from Sabrina to Caden's girlfriend, whose eyes bore into mine. I ticked my head toward the door as I glanced back to Sabrina. "I'm gonna head out."

She looked torn, as if I were asking her to choose and she wasn't sure whether she should stay or go.

"Don't worry. You stay," I assured her. "I'll just see you back at the dorm."

I could see the indecision in her eyes.

"I'm serious. I'll be fine."

She didn't look happy, but nodded nonetheless. We hadn't known each other long, but she clearly saw it was time for me to go.

I turned and headed out the front door, sucking in the fresh air as soon as I hit the porch. Some people sat out there concealed by darkness, their voices blending into the late night air. I made it down the front steps and onto the sidewalk with thoughts of the night's events on my mind. I'd had fun. I'd laughed. I'd felt like a real college girl for the first time since arriving on campus.

So why did I feel so guilty?

It was as if I'd been betraying Cole by having fun. By spending time with his teammates. By forgetting my hatred for Caden.

"Finlay."

My body jumped. I could hear Caden's footsteps on the pavement behind me approach.

"Where are you going?" He stepped in front of me causing me to stop.

The sight of him out there—when he had a house full of people—did weird things to my head. I found it difficult to match his gaze. "You were right. This isn't my scene."

He ducked his head to catch my eyes. "Weren't you having fun?"

Was it the uncertainty in his eyes? The hope that he wanted me to stay? Or just my confusion over both? Because tears unexpectedly blurred my vision.

"Don't leave." It came out so softly I couldn't even be sure he'd said it.

"What?"

As if he'd surprised himself, his face sobered. "You were having fun," he said, more detached and aloof, his eyes no longer on mine. "And you got the guys to have fun."

I stared at him, searching for the truth in his words. In his features. Was that the real reason he wanted me to stay? Had I just been his assistant for the night and nothing more? Were my confused feelings just one-sided? It was all too much—especially with my mind buzzed with alcohol. I knew enough to walk away. "I've got to get back to my dorm."

He dropped his gaze, and with pursed lips he nodded.

"I'll see you at practice." I turned to walk away.

"Wait."

I stopped, sucking in a deep breath.

"Let me take you home."

I twisted back around to face him. "You've got a house full of people and I've got two feet."

He cocked his head, my stubbornness an apparent thorn in his side.

"I'll be back to the dorm in no time," I assured him. "I'm fine."

He shot me a sad smile. "Promise me you'll be aware of your surroundings."

I nodded, recalling our run-in on the quad and him feeling the need to reprimand me even then. "Always."

With that, I headed toward my dorm without looking back. I would've heard his footsteps if he followed me. He hadn't. Why would he? He had a girlfriend.

CHAPTER TEN

Finlay

"I can't believe you're leaving again," Sabrina said as she walked in from her nightly shower.

I glanced up from the clothes I'd packed into my overnight bag. I needed to hurry if I was going to catch the nine o'clock bus for the overnight trip to Arkansas—our third road trip in as many weeks. "Sounds like you're gonna miss me?"

Sabrina dropped down onto her bed. "Damn right I am. Good thing I have pledge stuff to occupy my time. Oh, did I tell you? I got my big sister."

"No."

"Yeah. It's Leslie. The president."

"Caden's Leslie?"

She nodded, her eyes narrowing curiously. "Wait. Since when are you and Brooks on a first-name basis?"

I turned back to my bag and continued packing. "Brooks. Caden. It's whatever comes out."

"Uh-huh," she said unconvinced.

I shrugged. "Well, I'm happy for you."

"Yeah," she said. "I heard the president doesn't have to take a little sister. So I guess I'm honored she chose me. I didn't even think she knew who I was. But we got talking at the party and really hit it off."

"She seems…nice?"

"You don't sound sure."

I shrugged. "I don't know her. Caden seems to like her though."

"Yeah. She said they're already looking at million dollar houses for when he goes pro next year."

"Oh." An unwelcome pit formed in my stomach as I zipped up my overnight bag. Why were my feelings for him so freaking confusing? It should've been easy to keep hating him. But it had become harder with each passing day. It was as if he'd made up his mind and refused to allow me to.

Damn him.

* * *

Yvette had yet to arrive as I settled into the aisle seat. I reached into my backpack to find my tablet.

"Hey," Caden said, stepping out of the aisle and pushing his big body in front of me so I had to sit back.

"What are you doing?"

He dropped into the window seat beside me and flashed a devilish grin. "I need your help."

"Again?"

He laughed. "And she's cocky. Did I ever thank you for putting that game together at my house?"

"It was nothing," I said, my eyes jumping between him and the door. "Yvette will be here any minute."

"I'm sure Grady will give her a place to sit."

I pulled in a sharp breath. "Is something going on with them?"

He reached down and unzipped his backpack. "The only time I see the guy half-way decent is when he's talking to her. I should've invited her to my party." He sat up, holding his binder. "And so you know," he lowered his voice. "Coach gave me permission to sit here."

My brows pulled together. "Why?"

He held up his binder. "I need you to quiz me."

"Why can't Forester? He needs to know the plays, too."

"True..." His lips pulled up in one corner conspiratorially. "But he doesn't smell as good as you."

I cocked my head. "I bet there are quite a few girls who'd beg to differ."

He glanced over his shoulder, presumably at Forester, our star wide receiver who could seriously stop traffic. But it was more than his obvious sculptured body and dimples that drew attention from...well from everyone. It was the arrogant way he carried himself. The way a mere look from him said, 'Keep staring, ladies. I know I'm hot.'

"You got a thing for my roommate?" Caden asked, pulling me from my thoughts.

"What? Me? No."

He laughed, probably at the blush creeping into my cheeks. "Not into hot football players?"

My eyes narrowed on his. "You do realize you just called him hot, right?"

His low chuckle sent a slight vibration whizzing through me. "All right. I was joking. He smells fine."

"Now he's fine?"

He shook his head, probably at my inability to be the first one to back down from any sort of banter. "Fine."

"I know you just said that."

He reached up and placed his finger over my lips, not only silencing me but sending an unexpected tingle to my lips.

Shit.

"I sat here because I happen to know you have a stash of chocolate in that bag." He nodded toward my backpack on the floor as he removed his finger from my lips.

"How do you know that?"

He shrugged.

I wished I didn't like the fact that he paid attention to things like that or that my lips had yet to stop tingling. "Who said I'm sharing?"

"Oh, you're sharing all right."

I laughed, wishing he wasn't funny. Wishing he didn't smell so damn good up close. Wishing he didn't make my heart flip over itself when he said cute things. Wishing a lot of things when it came to Caden. And I hated myself for every single one.

Yvette boarded the bus, her eyes instantly training on Caden in her seat.

"It's all you," I said, tugging the playbook from his hand and flipping it open, wanting no part of explaining the seat change to Yvette.

Caden had no problem informing her the seat beside Grady was available. She actually stifled a grin and headed to it. "See?" he said.

"The girl can't be thinking straight. I mean, does he have a single redeeming quality?"

Caden laughed. "If he just focused on blocking and shutting his mouth, I wouldn't have a problem with him."

"That would be too easy." I glanced down at the open playbook in my lap. "Gold Hook."

"Throw an out pattern to Forester."

I rattled off another play. "Prince twenty-two."

"Hand off to Moore on the right."

"Yellow Fi—."

"Post route to the tight end," Caden answered before I even had a chance to finish.

"You sure you need my help? You seem to have these down."

His eyes drifted for a minute, staring out the darkened window at the field house we'd yet to depart from. When his eyes shifted back to me, they held indecision. His voice lowered again. "I struggle a little with remembering things."

I wasn't used to him being so vulnerable. So serious. "A lot of people struggle. You just need to figure out what works for you."

He nodded, his eyes appreciative. "The more I practice, the better I feel."

"Well, then, I guess we better keep at it."

A small smile curved his lips. "Why do you think I'm sitting next to the hottest girl on the bus asking for help?"

Normally, the compliment would've flushed my cheeks and caused my stomach to ripple something fierce, but since I knew except for Yvette, guys filled every other seat, I leveled Caden with my eyes. "Clever."

He laughed. "What? Am I lying?"

"Yvette's cute."

He cocked his head. "She's more Grady's type."

So what did that make me? "Black flag," I said, needing a subject change.

He smiled and the quizzing resumed for a good hour. At one point, I threw in psychology questions. He eyed me wearily.

"We've got a psych midterm in a couple weeks. Couldn't hurt to kill two birds with one stone."

He nodded. "I like the way you think."

"Actually," I said, pulling out my tablet. "This might help you. I found this app that lets you make quizzes for yourself."

He leaned over, looking down at my screen. "Are those flashcards?"

"Sort of."

He snickered. I wasn't sure if he was laughing because he thought it was immature to use flashcards in college or because he realized there were things available out there to help him. "I haven't used them since I was a kid."

"You're still a kid," I teased.

"Says the eighteen-year-old."

My eyes stayed on the screen as I clicked on the term *Conditioned Response*. The virtual card flipped to reveal the definition. "I'm not eighteen."

"Oh, sorry," he mocked. "*Nine*teen."

I shook my head, unprepared for where the conversation could take us. "I'll be twenty-one in January."

"Aren't you a freshman?"

I nodded, glancing over at him. "I took a couple years off."

His eyes widened in amusement. "To find yourself?"

Hmph. "Guess so."

"Did you find her?"

A rush of sadness flooded my body. "I'm not sure yet."

By two in the morning, the light above us was the only one on in the dark bus. We'd studied every possible play option—and psych term assigned this semester. He knew them. All of them. He had nothing to worry about—except, of course, whether or not his offensive line would come through for him or let Arkansas' defense have their way with him.

I handed him back his playbook which he tucked away in his bag.

"Now hand over more chocolate, woman."

I rolled my eyes as I reached into my diminishing stash of chocolate and dropped a handful into his palm.

"Thanks."

"Did I really have a choice? You would've wrestled me for them."

He snickered. "No, thanks for helping me."

I lifted a shoulder. "I didn't have a choice with that either."

He unwrapped a chocolate and popped it into his mouth. "Good point."

I leaned my head back against the headrest and closed my eyes. Caden's arm provided a nice support against my arm, his bigger body occupying more space than Yvette's. "Good night, Caden."

"Night, Finlay."

The purr of the bus's engine was a soothing melody, and in no time, it lulled me to sleep.

I awoke hours later when the bus jolted to a stop. It took a minute for my eyes to adjust to the sunlight outside as I lifted my head. I looked around the silent bus. Yvette was two seats back sound asleep on Grady's shoulder. I glanced to Caden beside me. His head rested against the window, his eyelashes fanned out over the tips of his cheeks.

The scraping of the door pulled my eyes from Caden and ignited stirring throughout the bus. Caden shifted, a yawn breaking free from him as his tired eyes slid to mine. "Morning," he rasped.

"Morning."

"How'd you sleep?" His bedhead made him look a lot younger than he normally did.

"Not bad."

"Me neither." He glanced down at his watch. "Made it to six. That's a record for me."

"Me too."

"I guess that solves our problem. If we're gonna sleep, it needs to be in a moving vehicle."

"Who knew?"

He smiled before scrubbing his hands over his face in an attempt to wake himself up.

The coaches in front of us began gathering their belongings. Coach Burns stood and faced us. "Start getting your things together. You can go in and get freshened up. We'll grab a light breakfast and then head to the stadium for practice."

"Thanks again for all your help," Caden whispered to me.

I shrugged as I reached for my bag. "It wasn't that bad."

"Sitting next to me?"

I cocked my head. "Helping you study. I like football."

"For a minute there I thought you were gonna say you like me."

"Don't get crazy now."

He laughed as his eyes drifted out the window and up the tall exterior of the hotel. "Wonder if they've got a pool."

I glanced out at the sleek building. "Probably."

He glanced back to me. "Then I expect a race this time. No running away."

"I wasn't running. I was scared you'd dunk me."

His face scrunched incredulously. "Why would I dunk you?"

I shrugged. "What else would you do?"

His eyes strayed back out the window. "I could think of a lot of things."

* * *

I watched practice from the sidelines. The offense looked like a cohesive unit for the first time all season. Grady, Lemer, and Miller hadn't missed a block all morning. I wondered if Grady spending the night beside Yvette had worked some type of magic and if my stellar game at Caden's party had done the trick for the others.

Speak of the devil. Pun definitely intended. Grady jogged to the sideline, his eyes searching me out. I approached him readily with a bottle of water and he tore it from my hand without a thank you. It was the moment I'd been waiting for, especially after his greeting at Caden's party.

As soon as he lifted the bottle to his mouth, I slipped a laxative bottle out of my pocket, making sure he could read the label as I pretended to skim the directions on it.

Grady spit his water all over the ground drawing a fair amount of attention from those around him.

I matched his gaze, my eyes blinking innocently as I slipped the bottle back into my pocket. I smiled as I turned and walked away, fairly confident Grady wouldn't be busting my chops anymore.

I glanced out at the field as Grady returned to his position. Caden got the ball and dropped back in the pocket, seeking out a receiver. Grady and the line held their ground, not allowing anyone through. They were ready for Arkansas. I could see it. In every pass completion and every block. Arkansas wouldn't know what hit them.

* * *

I crept into the dark indoor pool area with my towel wrapped around me. It was three in the morning and I figured if I beat Caden down there, I could slip into the water before him.

"You're early," his deep voice echoed through the room.

My body stilled as my eyes shot around, trying to adapt to the darkness.

"Can't you see me?" This time his voice sounded like it was beside me.

I twisted around, searching the darkness.

"Nope. Not there."

I twisted back, searching the surface of the water as well as the empty lounge chairs. *Okay.* This was ridiculous. I dropped my towel and walked to the edge of the pool in my green bikini, diving in before he had a chance to push me in. It was surprisingly refreshing for a heated pool. When I surfaced, a splash to my right sprayed water up around me. I moved myself to the edge and hung on, my eyes scanning the surface.

Caden broke through the water a few feet away, rotating to find me. His eyes latched on to mine. "Still scared I'm gonna dunk you?"

"Let's just say I know I'm safer over here."

He laughed. "You have no idea."

The assurance in his raspy voice twisted my insides.

"Sorry we didn't get to talk at practice."

My face wrinkled in confusion. "When do we ever talk at practice?"

He made his way over to the edge and held on with one arm. "I just didn't want you to think you were like other girls."

"Okay, you've completely lost me." Had it not been so dark, I would've had difficulty averting my gaze from the corded muscles in his arm as he held himself in place.

He smirked. "Did we or did we not spend the night together?"

I rolled my eyes. "I guess technically we did."

"Exactly. I didn't want you to think I was the kind of guy who doesn't call."

I smiled. "Oh, so you're funny?"

He laughed. "Some people think so."

"Then you should surround yourself with them at all times."

His eyes turned to slits. "Why?"

"Because I'm sure they think everything you say and do is just spot on because you're Alabama's quarterback."

"So you're saying everyone who laughs at my jokes does it because I can throw a football?"

"Sorry to break it to you, but you're not very funny."

He snickered. "Tell me how you really feel."

I shook my head. "That would take way too long."

He lowered himself under water for a second then resurfaced a little closer to me. He gripped the wall with one arm as his eyes dropped to my lips. "I like your honesty."

My traitorous breaths became shallow. "Even when it's directed at you?"

"Especially when it's directed at me." He pushed his wet hair off his forehead. "Never be afraid to tell people what you're really thinking. It's one of the most refreshing things about you."

I nodded. "I'll have to remember that when you're throwing like a girl."

He stifled a smile. "I wouldn't expect anything less." He paused, a contemplative look in his eyes. "You know, you're really easy to talk to."

"As opposed to your teammates? Because I've heard some of their conversations. And there's some pretty deep stuff going on there."

He laughed to himself, probably recalling the latest story about the kicker's weekend conquest—the entire pledge class of Delta house. And for some reason, when Caden laughed like that, in a way that hit me deep, I found it impossible to remember why everything about us being there together was so wrong. My eyes zoned in on his lips. I never really looked at them before. But glazed with pool water they looked so damned kissable.

Caden cleared his throat.

My eyes jumped to his. He stared at me with a deep intensity. One that beckoned me closer. I felt myself involuntarily being pulled toward him, my eyes dropping to his mouth again. Wondering what it would be like to just press my lips to his. I could feel his breath against my face as he too moved closer. My eyes fluttered shut as I moved the last inch necessary to kiss him.

"Leslie," Caden whispered.

My eyes snapped open. That one word sent me scampering back as if I'd been doused with a bucket of ice water. "Oh, God." I turned and, holding onto the wall with one arm and trying to swim with the other, I splashed my way to the closest ladder, unable to swim as quickly as necessary to escape the humiliation I'd brought upon myself. *Stupid. Stupid. Stupid.*

"Finlay," Caden called.

I climbed out of the pool and rushed to the chair that held my towel. "I've gotta get back to my room. I—"

"Wait."

I wrapped the towel around me, clutching it tightly—as if it could somehow protect me from the embarrassment consuming every part of my body. I just wanted to crawl into a ball and disappear. "I'm so sorry." I spun around and practically ran out of the pool area and through the lobby to the elevator. The forty seconds it took for the elevator to hit the ground floor and for the doors to open was forty seconds too long. Caden stepped up beside me.

Shit. Shit. Shit.

He stood back, letting me enter first. "After you."

I stepped inside. The cool air chilled my damp skin as I pressed my body into the corner, unable to get as far away from him as I needed to. Caden stepped inside. The towel wrapped around his waist left me face-to-face with his wet bare chest.

Fan-freaking-tastic.

He turned and pressed the button for our floor. As soon as the doors closed, the electricity inside was palpable. I averted my gaze, focusing on anything but him.

Caden turned, towering over me even more so now that I was barefoot and pressed into the corner of the already small space. "I just wanna—"

I held up my palm, my eyes dropping to my feet. "If you care about me even the tiniest bit, you'll stop whatever it is you're gonna say."

"Okay."

I glanced up, trying desperately to keep my eyes from venturing to his chest, as I exhaled the mother of all breaths. "Thank you."

"And for what it's worth," he said. "I do."

I met his gaze. "What?"

"I do care about you."

This time my breath was slow and elongated, the effect of his words and apologetic expression. *Oh, God.* Did he pity me?

The tight space suddenly felt like it was closing in on us.

The elevator stopped on our floor and the doors opened. I raced out mumbling something about seeing him later. I didn't breathe again until I stepped into my room and was locked safely inside.

CHAPTER ELEVEN

Finlay

I stared dumbstruck from the sideline as the trainers rushed onto the field. The crowd stood deathly silent. Caden had been down for no more than twenty seconds, but the hit that brought him to the ground was delivered by two of Arkansas' biggest defensive backs, tackling him from both sides. Somehow, the crushing of his bones was heard over the roar of the crowd. If something wasn't broken, it'd be a miracle.

I stood helplessly while the trainers knelt over his motionless body.

Two minutes passed as they spoke to a seemingly unresponsive Caden. I watched their faces. Watched for fear in their eyes. Watched for any indication as to whether or not they thought he'd be okay.

They gave nothing away.

After another thirty seconds, Caden's helmet moved to the side on its own accord.

A giant whoosh of relief broke through my lips. I watched the same relief extend over on the trainers' faces. I wondered if they feared the worst like me or if they expected it to be a routine wind-knocked-out-of-him situation.

They quickly leaned down, speaking to Caden over the noise in the stadium. One of them grasped his right leg and brought it up toward his thigh, bending it slightly at the knee. I wished he would've shoved off his helmet. I wished I could've seen his face to know how serious his pain was. But it remained on.

An ambulance drove out of the tunnel and over to our sideline. Everyone's attention moved to the EMT's pulling a gurney from the back. The trainers surrounding Caden held up their palms to hold them off. They said something to Caden then they nodded in understanding. Within minutes, they'd lifted him slowly to his feet. Applause from Arkansas' fans filled the stadium. Caden put minimal pressure on his right foot as they gingerly walked him off the field. Once they reached the bench on our sideline, a golf cart drove over. They helped him onto the back and the cart sped off, taking him to the locker room for what I assumed would be a mandatory evaluation.

For the remainder of the game I did nothing but bite my fingernails and watch the game clock tick slowly down. Caden hadn't returned, nor had the medical staff. Palmer, Caden's back-up, was doing a fine job handing off passes quickly. Coach clearly didn't want to risk him suffering the same fate as Caden up against such a ferocious defense.

I knew it was irrational given what happened in the pool, but I needed to get into the locker room to see if he was okay. After seeing him unconscious, the reasons I'd hated him so much in the beginning didn't seem so important anymore. He'd been nothing but kind to me. I don't know what made him smile at Cole's wake, but that wasn't the guy I'd gotten to know. The guy I'd tried to kiss.

When the game ended and we somehow recorded a win, I hurried into the locker room, my eyes shooting around. Caden was nowhere to be found, nor were the trainers. Minutes ticked by as I waited for the coaches to file out of Coach Burns' temporary office after their post-game meeting. Then I slipped inside. Coach's head lifted from the papers in front of him.

"How is he?" I asked.

"I'm heading to the hospital right now to see for myself."

My eyes jumped around the office. Arkansas burgundy surrounded us. My eyes settled uncomfortably back on Coach Burns. "Mind if I come with you?"

He stared back at me. The fear in my eyes must've been a stark reminder to him that I'd lost my brother on a football field. That I wasn't there the day he died. That I wasn't like everyone else. Things affected me differently than other people.

Coach's lips pressed into a tight line before he nodded.

Caden

"You look like shit."

With my head pounding like a motherfucker, it took some effort, but my eyes opened slowly. I almost smiled at the sight of Finlay in the chair beside my hospital bed. If it had to be someone, I was glad it was Finlay and not any of the guys. They would've bombarded me with questions about my injuries and made me feel like a dick for getting hurt. "Thanks," I mumbled, wondering how long I'd been asleep and how long she'd been there. Machines beeped around me. Wires were attached to my arms and chest. And my body still ached liked a son of a bitch.

"So, what's the diagnosis?" she asked nonchalantly, though the quiver in her voice told me she was worried.

"Pulled quad muscle."

"Nothing's broken?" Her voice was incredulous.

"Don't sound so surprised."

"I heard your bones crack."

"It looked worse than it was." I couldn't tell her how much my leg ached. I couldn't tell anyone. At least it wasn't my arm. "Fucking Grady missed the block."

"We've got to get him and Yvette together," she said matter-of-factly.

"What?"

"Sitting next to her on the bus earned you a great practice. The guy looked amazing out there. Just think how he'd do in a game if they were getting busy."

"Getting busy?" I choked out a laugh. How the fuck could I laugh at a time like that?

Finlay smiled at her own corniness, and I liked that she had.

"You think she'll be that explosive in the sack?"

She shrugged. "It's always the quiet ones."

I raised a brow. "Is it now?"

Her mouth parted, before she stumbled all over her words. "Well…I…I think she needs a push." She slipped out her phone. "I'll let her know I'm not coming back to the room."

Oh, this was getting good. "Where you gonna be?"

She glanced up from her phone. "I can stay in the lobby."

"Don't be ridiculous. Stay here."

Her brows shot up. "Here?" Her eyes appraised my single room. "This chair isn't exactly comfortable."

I patted the mattress beside me. "I have a perfectly comfortable bed right here."

Instead of the amusement I anticipated, anger clouded her green eyes. "Says the guy with the girlfriend who'd likely kick his ass if she found out he shared a bed with a girl who wasn't her."

The cold clip to her voice and the way she glared at me with disdain pissed me the hell off. I thought she'd moved past whatever irked her about me. And, God dammit, she was the one who damn near kissed *me* the previous night. If anyone had forgotten I had a girlfriend, it was her. "I'd never cheat."

Finlay's eyes splayed. "I wasn't implying—"

"I'm not like that," I said, cutting her off.

She shook her head. "I didn't say you were."

"I'd break up with someone before I ever cheated."

"Fine." Finlay shuffled in her seat, clearly uncomfortable with the direction our conversation had taken. A long silence passed before she spoke again. "I brought your stuff."

I spotted my bag on the floor beside her chair. "Thanks."

She nodded before another long silence passed between us. "Have you spoken to your family?"

I shook my head. "I'm a big boy."

She rolled her eyes. "That's what they all say."

I reached for the tie on the hospital gown they made me wear, calling her bluff. "Care to find out?"

Her mouth opened then closed just as quickly. I loved unnerving her. "Coach'll be here any minute. He's talking to your doctors right now," she said, trying to stop me from disrobing.

I nodded, inwardly laughing at how flustered she got at the thought of seeing me naked. "He's got to make sure his investment can play."

She cocked her head, her eyes searching my face. "You do realize he cares about you, right? He didn't rush over here as soon as the game ended to make sure his *investment* was okay. He rushed here to make sure his *player* was okay."

"How do you know?"

She shrugged, and for the first time it seemed like she was hiding something. Like she knew something I didn't know. "He's a good man."

My lips twisted as I considered her certainty. He was a good man. And a great coach. But football was a business, and he played his part, knowing his job depended on whether we won or lost. He needed me out there. "So why are *you* here?"

"Are you kidding? I'm making sure my investment doesn't blow it and take the rest of the team down with him."

I laughed. "*Your* investment?"

"I'm invested in whether you win or lose. *And* your quest to bring the idiots together. It wasn't a job I'd planned on. But I'm gonna make sure I follow it through to the end."

I loved her ability to joke while keeping a straight face. "I'm glad you're here."

She nodded, quietly fidgeting with the hem of her Alabama T-shirt.

"So, what are our plans for tonight?"

Her eyes flashed up, determined and serious. "*If* I decide to stay here, which I haven't agreed to yet—"

"Yet," I repeated, earning me a cocked head.

"I plan on sitting right here and talking to your sorry ass until the pain meds knock you out again. I'm hoping that's sooner rather than later." She laughed, and when she laughed like that, it made me look at her in a whole different light. One that showed authenticity and carried a calmness with it, blanketing everyone around her, including me, in a safe little bubble.

Finlay

My elbow slipped off the armrest for the umpteenth time, jarring me from an uncomfortable sleep.

"Finlay, I swear to you. I'm not gonna try anything." My eyes moved to Caden in his hospital bed, reclined in an almost upright position even though the sun was hours from rising. "Just come up here," he said.

I glanced to the white sheets covering him from the waist down. He'd opted for a pair of practice shorts and a sleeveless shirt that of course molded to every indentation in his chest, not to mention displayed his jacked biceps.

"I'll stay under the blankets. You can stay on top," he assured me.

I tilted my head, picturing myself on the bed with him. What if someone walked in? What if a reporter got a photo? What if being that close to him made me feel things I'd hate myself for feeling? "The chair's fine."

"Bullshit. Now you're either coming up here on your own or I'll drag my beaten ass out of bed and carry you."

I stared back at him. Why couldn't a single guy—one I hadn't sworn to loathe for eternity—proposition me like that? Why couldn't anything in my life be that easy? "Fine." I pushed my exhausted body to my feet and turned my back to the bed, trying unsuccessfully to scoot into the space beside him. I glanced over my shoulder. "Are you gonna move over?"

"Didn't realize you'd have a problem lying on top of me."

I glared at him, trying to disguise my amusement. "I hate you."

He laughed as he shifted over a couple inches, careful of his leg as he moved. "I think you want to hate me, but you can't resist the charm."

I rolled my eyes as I settled in, kicking my feet up and reclining against his heap of pillows. My eyes strayed to the television. Recaps of the day's college football games flashed on the screen. "How many times have they shown your injury?"

"Too many."

"Yeah." I winced at the recollection. "Once was enough for me, too. It was pretty scary."

"Yeah, my nose ending up like Grady's was definitely scary for me, too." He knew that wasn't what I meant, but his confidence wouldn't allow him to show even a sliver of vulnerability. It made me wonder if he was in more pain than he was letting on.

More replays flashed on the muted television as we watched them in silence.

Way too quickly, Caden's presence became all-consuming. He was a big guy, more so in a small hospital bed with his bicep and leg pressed against mine. His steady breathing just inches away from me invaded my subconscious. The rising and falling of his chest taunted me, reminding me this was the first bed I'd shared with a guy in two years. And this guy was charming and maddening rolled up into one hot package. The rugged scent rolling off him seeped into my pores, permeating all my senses. That was it. I needed a distraction. I needed noise. "So, what's the deal with the draft?"

His head turned on the pillow. With his blue eyes zeroed in on mine, I realized just how close we were. And the breath I'd only been listening to was now fanning over my face. "Thanks for asking."

"What?"

"No one but you and Coach have asked. They all just assume."

Feeling awkward being so close with his attention solely on me, my eyes wandered back to the television. A quarterback being sacked in another game filled the screen. "I've learned never to assume anything in life."

"You're smart."

"Obviously."

His quiet laughter shook the bed. "Teams have shown interest."

I looked back to him, but his eyes had shifted to the television. "Of course they have. You're a great player."

He scoffed. "When my line's not getting me crushed."

"Yeah, but a great quarterback will figure out how to make the plays without them screwing it up."

"When you've got three-hundred-pound linemen out for your blood and you've got no coverage, it's easier said than done."

He needed to stop blaming other people, even if they were the cause. Cole would've figured out another way to make it work. He never would've given up.

"I don't know if I'm ready for the pros."

His words surprised me. "Why's that?"

"Playing for Alabama has always been my dream, ever since I was a kid."

My heart ached, knowing he and Cole shared that dream.

"After this year, I only have one year left at school," he continued. "I'm not sure I want to give that up."

"Not for the fame and fortune of playing in the pros?"

He looked at me with narrowed eyes. "I don't care about any of that. I care about the game. And my love for the game. Once it's my job, I can't say I'll love it the same."

Wow. Never in my wildest dreams did I think I'd hear that from him. I almost wished I hadn't. It just made me like him more. "There are risks in playing another year. I mean…" My eyes drifted around the small hospital room. "...look where you are. Next time, it might be worse. And then the pros won't even be an option."

He nodded. "I know the risks."

Cole would've been just as stubborn. He would have stayed another year, knowing the risks and wanting to prove everyone else wrong. "How long do they think you'll be out?"

"I'll play next week. They'll pump me with cortisone shots and I'll be fine."

"What about your head?"

"Hasn't failed me so far," he said with all the innate confidence in the world.

I sniggered, quite certain I knew which head he was referring to.

His phone vibrated on the nightstand, drawing my attention to it. When he didn't move to grab it, I glanced to him. "You gonna get that?"

He shook his head.

"It might be your parents."

He shrugged.

"Don't you want to talk to them?"

His eyes cut to mine, staring for a long time before speaking. "My mom's in California."

"I'm sure she'd be on the next flight out. Maybe she already is."

He shook his head. "I already talked to her. Told her not to bother. I'll be out of the hospital tomorrow."

"You don't want her here?"

"I don't want her worrying. She's had enough bad shit happen to her in this lifetime. Don't want to add to it."

Though I didn't know what he was referring to, I understood the notion of not wanting to burden others when they were in just as bad a place as you.

The silent television played as we lay there for a long time. Nurses walked by, some poking their heads in to check on him while others rushed by to see other patients.

"My dad's a dick," Caden said out of nowhere.

My head fell toward his, but he wasn't looking at me. "What?"

"My dad. He's a world class asshole. He won't call, but I guarantee he'll show up here trying to look like father of the year. I'm surprised he hasn't already."

"I'm sorry."

He shrugged like it was no big deal, but the anger in his voice said otherwise.

"No, I'm sorry you got gypped in the dad department."

He looked to me and, for the first time, I saw a heaviness plaguing his eyes. "I've never really talked about him to anyone before."

"Well, I'm glad it was me. Because I can promise you one thing. I'll hate him just for you."

His lips formed a sad smile as his phone vibrated again. Still, he ignored it, his eyes moving back to the television.

I watched a couple minutes of the game recaps before my eyelids became heavy, and the darkness in his room slowly pulled me into sleep.

Caden

"Son?"

I jolted up, startling Finlay who'd fallen asleep on my shoulder. We both sprang up disoriented.

"Oh, my God," Finlay said, throwing her legs off the bed as soon as she realized where she was.

"What are you doing here?" I didn't even try hiding my disgust as I glared at my father and his wife standing in the doorway.

Finlay's eye's shot to mine, realizing I'd totally called my father's move.

"You were hurt. And your coach called," my father explained, like it wasn't some big act.

"Which was it? I was hurt or Coach called?"

He huffed in exasperation, his expected reaction when I asked a question he had no comeback for. "I'm driving you back to campus. You need to extend your leg which you can't do on the bus."

"I'm fine."

Finlay jumped to her feet, grabbing her backpack from the floor as she high-tailed it to the door.

"Where do you think you're going?" I asked.

She looked back at me, her body tense and her words cautious. "I've got to get back if I'm gonna catch the bus home."

"Oh, no you don't. If I'm driving back, so are you." She opened her mouth to respond, but I cut her off. "I'll call Coach."

"Caden, really. The bus is fine."

"You're really going to deny me this?" I was totally milking my injury for all it was worth.

She cocked her head, visibly holding her tongue in front of my father and his wife. Her eyes danced across my face, indecision written all over her pretty features. I would've given anything to know what she was really thinking. "Fine. But I need a coffee," she grumbled as she turned and walked through the door. Something stopped her in her tracks and she glanced over her shoulder. "First tell me how you're feeling."

A slow smile slipped across my face. Of course she'd ask. "Better now."

She rolled her eyes and shook her head as she walked out of the room mumbling to herself.

A feeling of triumph swept over me as I watched her disappear into the hallway. Ignoring my father completely, I grabbed my phone from the nightstand. Leslie had been blowing up my phone all night, but I just didn't know what to say to her. Especially with Finlay there and it feeling way too right. Like it's how it should have been.

Leslie's presence wouldn't have brought me the same calm Finlay's did. And that was the thought that plagued my mind as Finlay lay asleep on my shoulder and I had all the time in the world to think. About the almost kiss. About the way her presence made me feel. About the fact that she'd come to my aide.

More than once I found myself burying my nose in her hair and inhaling the scent of her coconut shampoo. It was all I could focus on. That's not true.

The side of her body pressed against mine required focus and control to keep my body in check. More than once I had to think of my stats to keep my morning wood from embarrassing me if she woke up early. And her lips. I had no clue how I hadn't just kissed the fuck out of her with her face so close to mine. Just like in the pool, the man upstairs was definitely testing my resolve.

And even if nothing was actually going on with Finlay and me, I knew I needed to be around her. I knew I needed more time with her.

"Son?" My father's voice snapped me out of my head. "Maybe you should let her ride back with the team. We could use the time to talk."

I glanced up. The gray hair around his ears had spread since I'd seen him last. He'd shown up at one of my games last year, meeting me outside the locker room after the win. I made it known in no uncertain terms that he wasn't welcome there. Someone who'd shown so little respect for my mother didn't deserve mine. "There's nothing you could say to me that someone else couldn't hear."

He ground his teeth, the tick in his jaw prominent as I lifted my phone to my ear. "Hey Coach…yeah I'm feeling good…Yup. He just showed up. Said he's taking me back…I hope you don't mind, but I offered to take Finlay back with us…Yeah…I will." I looked to my father and held out my phone. "He wants to talk to you."

He took the phone and walked out into the hallway.

His wife stared at me with the same disappointed look my own mother would've given me. "He's been really worried about you."

"That's funny. I was under the impression he only worried about himself."

She closed her eyes for a long moment, clearly needing strength to deal with me. "He made a mistake years ago, Caden. We both did. But we're together now. We have a family. Can't you just look beyond the past and let him be part of your future? Let us both be part of it."

My eyes narrowed on this woman who destroyed my family. Everything about her perfect hair and pant suit disgusted me. "Do you want to know why I can't look past it? Why I will never have a relationship with that man or you? Because I have this thing called loyalty. And it's to my mother. Not him. And certainly not you."

She nodded, a million thoughts playing across her face. "It must be nice to live in your world," she said softly. "A world where everything is so black and white." She paused for a long time, before she pinned me with her eyes. "Be sure to say hello to your girlfriend for us. Leslie, isn't it?" She didn't bother saying another word as she turned and walked out of my room.

It was as if I'd been leveled by a freight train moving at full speed. By the realization. By the fact that *she* had to be the one to point out what I already knew.

I'd been treading a very fine line with Finlay. A line that—had I crossed it—I never would've been able to return from it. I'd spent the last ten years swearing I'd never be my father. And there I was nearly following in the same damn footsteps. What started off innocent had become much more serious. How had I not realized it? How had I let it happen?

The one thing I had going for me was I wasn't my father. I wouldn't cross that line. I was better than him. And if I wasn't, I'd make damn sure to change that.

I grabbed for the room phone beside me and dialed, lifting the large corded receiver to my ear. She answered on the first ring. "Hey, Leslie."

"Oh my God, Caden. You haven't been answering your phone." She sounded so relieved. "How are you?"

A knot formed in my gut, twisting my insides. "I'm okay."

"It looked really bad. They kept talking about it and replaying it."

"Yeah, well, it's just a pulled quad muscle. I'll play next week," I assured her, though I wondered if I was trying to assure myself.

"They're making it sound like a career ending injury." It wasn't a question, but it might as well have been.

"Nope. I'll be fine."

"Thank God," she sighed.

I wondered what she would've done if my injury was career ending. If I was just an average college student who didn't play a sport. If my future career was an accountant or a banker who couldn't afford those million dollar homes her daddy sold and she kept thrusting in my face. Why was she with me in the first place? Was it because I was the starting quarterback? Was it because I might've gone pro? We really had nothing in common aside from a great sex life. Why hadn't I realized that before?

"When are you coming home?" she asked.

I pulled in a deep breath, staring at the muted television playing in front of me, still reeling from my stepmother's words. "Not sure."

"Well, I miss you."

A heavy silence descended. It was a sobering moment to realize—with much certainty—that I hadn't missed her. I never missed her when I was away. But the short time Finlay had left me alone in my room, I'd been wondering when *she'd* return. I knew I needed to be honest with Leslie. I needed to be honest with myself. If I didn't come clean, I would've been just as deceitful as my father. "Listen, Leslie." I somehow stopped myself from following it up with, 'we need to talk.'

"What?" She sounded apprehensive.

"I need to say something, and I know you're not going to understand. And I'm sorry."

"Okay, you're starting to scare me," she said through nervous laughter.

"I can't do this anymore."

"Do what?"

I paused to garner my nerve. "Us."

Silence filled Leslie's end like I knew it would. I was stupid to do it over the phone. But after seeing my father. Seeing his wife. Thinking about the hurt they caused. The destruction they'd done. I knew it wasn't fair to be spending time with Finlay and thinking about her the way I increasingly was. It just solidified that what Leslie and I had wasn't right.

"Uh, huh." She sounded unconvinced. "I'll play along. Why? Why all of a sudden are you deciding this?"

I dropped my head back against the pillow and stared up at the ceiling. "It's just not right."

"Not right? What's not right?"

I stayed silent, trying to decide how to make it clear to her without hurting her more than I already was.

"Caden. Are you on medication? Because this sounds like the medication talking."

"It's not."

"I don't believe you. This is coming out of left field. Why would it be the first time you're mentioning it?"

I hated hurting people. It wasn't in my nature. But I needed to make it so she had no doubt. If I didn't, her fucking inquisition would've never ended. "I have feelings for someone else."

She gasped. I could almost see the claws coming out. "Who?"

"What?"

Her disbelief quickly transformed to anger. "Don't give me that bullshit, Caden. Who the hell is she?"

I paused. I didn't want to bring it up. I just wanted to bow out as respectfully as I could without hurting her, but she was making it damn near impossible.

"I asked you a fucking question you son of a bitch."

Her words couldn't hurt me as much as the realization that I almost headed down a path like my father. "It doesn't matter."

"Of course it matters."

"She doesn't even know. It's just…I shouldn't be thinking about anyone else while I'm with you."

There was silence. Had she hung up? Was she crying? "You're not thinking straight," she said, breaking the long silence. "We'll talk about it when you get back and you're not so out of it."

"Leslie," I said, this time sterner. "Would you rather me drag this out? I want to be up front with you. Can't you respect that?"

"I'll see you when you get back." And just like that, she disconnected the call.

I closed my eyes. Of course it wasn't going to be that easy. It had been a rash decision to do it like that. It wasn't the way I wanted it to go down. But it needed to end. Her push for us to buy a house together after dating for six fucking months, my father's unwelcome visit, and his wife's words pushed me over the edge. And even though Finlay and I didn't even have a real relationship, I knew it was wrong to stay with Leslie. I wouldn't be my dad. I'd never be him.

"Hey."

My eyes sprang open.

Finlay stood in my doorway with her backpack on her back and two smoothies in her hands. It looked like she'd tamed her dark waves while she'd been gone. She didn't need makeup. She didn't need much of anything. She was the girl-next-door and that was hot as hell. "Am I interrupting something?"

I shook my head as I hung up the phone, a calmness sweeping over me now that she'd returned. "Nope."

She walked in, placing a smoothie on the nightstand beside me. "Your dad's talking to your doctor. He told me to give you this." She pulled my phone from her pocket and handed it to me.

"Thanks." I grabbed the smoothie. "How do you know what flavor I like?"

"I Googled it." She dropped down into the chair. "You can find out a lot about a superstar like you on the Internet." She sucked down a long sip of her smoothie.

I laughed, my eyes mesmerized by her damn lips puckered around the tip of the straw. "Oh yeah? What's my favorite color?"

"Red."

I laughed. "Lucky guess. Do I rock boxers or briefs?"

"So easy," she said with a knowing smirk. "Briefs."

"That's really on there?"

She shook her head. "I've seen your ass more times than I care to admit in the locker room. And don't act like you don't do it on purpose to give me a show."

I laughed as I sipped my own smoothie. Strawberry. My favorite. I lifted my phone and tapped the screen, searching a couple sites then dialing the number I'd been looking for. When the person on the other end answered, I rattled off instructions while Finlay stared at me, her eyes ready to burst out of her head. She wanted to strangle me. Was it weird that I might've enjoyed it? I disconnected the call.

"You can't do that," she said, a cross between awe and fear in her voice.

"Watch me."

Her lips tightened into an angry thin line as she shook her head. "I can't do that."

"Of course you can. Just blame me. What's the worst that could happen?"

"Seriously? Do you want the list?"

I smiled. She was fucking adorable when she worried like that. And I suddenly couldn't wait to spend the next nine hours with her.

CHAPTER TWELVE

Finlay

He was freaking nuts. That's what ran through my head as I stood in the hospital lobby with keys to a rental car in my hand. We were going to be in so much trouble. Not only would his father call Coach, but what the hell was I going to do for almost nine hours in a car alone with him? It was bad enough sleeping next to him all night, inhaling his amazing scent. Listening to the soft hum of his breath. The rhythm of his heartbeat.

But now?

How was I supposed to remain unfazed by his charm? His good looks? *Him*?

The elevator doors parted and a pretty nurse pushed Caden toward me in a wheelchair. Of course he'd get the pretty one. She probably paid one of the older nurses for the privilege. But the smile on his face wasn't directed at her. It was directed at me. "Can you seriously not walk?" I asked when they stopped in front of me.

He grabbed the crutches that lay across his lap and stood, using them to support his body while babying his right leg. “It’s sore. I just need to stay off it and keep it extended.”

“So, you’re going to sprawl out in the back seat while I cart your ass across state lines?”

He grinned. “That’s the plan.”

There was a lightness to his words. To his features. To his eyes. It was as if something had changed now that he didn’t have to spend hours in a car with his father.

“Well, you might want to get moving,” I said. “Your dad’s probably almost finished with lunch.”

He laughed as the entrance doors slid apart and he hobbled outside on his crutches, stopping at the maroon four-door sedan parked at the curb. He glanced over at me. “Aren’t you gonna get the door?”

I walked around to the driver’s side. “When hell freezes over.”

“Don’t sound so high and mighty. You’re my accomplice.”

“Your *unwilling* accomplice. That’s what I plan to tell Coach.” I slid into the driver’s seat and started the engine.

“Did I use a weapon?” Caden asked, maneuvering himself into the backseat.

“Several.”

He laughed as he closed the door and settled in.

I pulled away from the curb, clearing the parking lot and heading out onto the main road.

“Thanks for doing this,” he said, the sincerity in his voice taking me aback.

“Don’t thank me yet. I failed my driver’s test three times.”

“Bullshit.”

I shook my head. "Nope. Hit a curb the first time. Went the wrong way down a one-way street the second. And I nearly clipped two kids in a crosswalk the third."

His laughter filled the car. "That's fucking hysterical."

"For you maybe. Having my br—" *Shit.* "Having my dad drive me around, not so much."

"Well, if you just warn me before making an abrupt stop, we should be fine."

I nodded. "I can do that." My navigation instructed me to turn left and remain on that road for the next hundred and fourteen miles.

"I bet right now my father's threatening to sue every person in that hospital."

I glanced at him through the rearview mirror. "Do you care?"

He shook his head. "Nope."

"Do you mind me asking what happened between the two of you?"

He paused for a long time, staring out the window at the passing trees. I wondered if he trusted me enough to tell me. To divulge his family issues. To let me in. "He cheated on my mom."

My chest tightened around my heart. "I'm sorry."

"Nothing for you to be sorry about. He did it. He broke my mom's heart. And then left us."

"You don't talk to him?"

"Not unless I have to. Like today. But otherwise, it's pretty easy to write someone off after they do something like that."

I nodded, understanding—as mortifying as it was—his reaction in the pool even more.

"I'll never be like him."

Our eyes met in the rearview mirror and the honesty in them mixed with something else. Something he clearly wanted me to understand. My eyes jumped back to the rural Arkansas road in front of me. There was one thing I knew for sure. The road was a lot less dangerous than those blue eyes. And their owner.

Caden

"So…no boyfriend?" I asked from my spot in the backseat a little while later.

Finlay glanced at me through the rearview mirror, her green eyes locking on mine. "Do you think any guy could handle this?"

I smirked. "He'd be a fool not to try."

I could see my words unnerved her in the way her eyes flashed back to the road and she readjusted in her seat. "Well, most guys don't want an independent girl."

"Not true. I enjoy a challenge."

"Your girlfriend does seem pretty strong-willed."

"Strong-willed? Is that your way of saying she's a bitch?"

Finlay's eyes widened. "No. I don't even know her."

I laughed. "I'm just joking. She was definitely strong-willed."

"Was?"

"We broke up."

Her head recoiled, her eyes still on the road. "Oh. I'm sorry. I didn't know."

I shrugged. "It just happened."

"That's too bad."

"Is it?" I stared into the mirror, waiting for her to look at me, to show some sign that the news affected her in some way. But her eyes remained on the road.

"Like I said," I continued, hoping she understood what I was saying. "I'd never cheat."

Her eyes flashed up, our gazes colliding in the mirror.

I almost laughed at the fright in her eyes. But I couldn't relent. Not yet anyway. "Do you think you can drive all the way through or should we find a place to crash at some point?"

Her eyes rounded. "Oh…uh…"

Oh, this was getting good. For someone so strong, someone who had a comeback for everything, I'd definitely tongue-tied her.

"I think I'll be fine."

"You say that now, but when it's dark and you've been staring at the same, long, dark road, you're gonna be seeing double."

Finlay said nothing.

If I was being honest, her not jumping at the chance to spend the night with me in a hotel room—now that I'd made it clear I was single—definitely hurt my ego. But I guess it wouldn't have been Finlay if she didn't challenge me and make me work for it.

Finlay

The sunlight on the horizon threatened to blind me with its fierceness as afternoon morphed into evening. I sang along to the country songs on the radio while Caden slept in the backseat. He'd been out for hours, clearly not getting much sleep in the hospital. I envied him, as my eyes stung from the hours staring at the open road. When my navigation announced our destination on the right, anxious butterflies danced in my belly. I could not wait to get there.

I pulled to an abrupt stop by the sidewalk, purposely jostling the car. Caden stirred in the backseat, the movement jarring him from sleep. "Are we home?" he asked, sitting up and looking out the window all sleepy and disoriented. "Wait. Where are we?"

I stifled a grin. "Topela."

"Topela?" he asked, like he'd never heard of it. I was fairly certain he hadn't.

"Yeah, Topela, Mississippi. Elvis' birthplace. Thought we'd take the scenic route." I had no idea how I managed not to burst out laughing as I pushed open my door. It was probably my desperate need to stand and stretch my stiff legs *and* find a restroom.

Caden's door squeaked open and his crutches hit the pavement, assisting him out of the backseat. "Is that why we're here?" He lifted his chin toward the statue in front of Topela City Hall.

"Yup." I walked the hundred or so feet over to it with a huge smile on my face.

After the minute it took for him to catch up, Caden stepped beside me, his eyes moving over the tall bronze statue of Elvis atop a large pedestal. It was an amazing replica of him leaning forward with his right leg bent and his right hand out, as if reaching down to his screaming fans. His lips were rounded as he sang into the old-time microphone on the stand in front of him, it too leaning with his forward movement. "So you're an Elvis fan?"

"Isn't everyone?" I asked, having a little fun with him.

He shrugged. "Given all your singing, I should've known you liked country music."

I jerked a glance over at him. "You heard me?"

"Yeah. You're terrible."

I laughed. "I can't believe you just said that."

"Would you rather I lie?"

I rolled my eyes. "No. But now that I know how you feel about it, I plan on singing even louder just for you."

He snickered as he pointed to a spot right in front of the statue. "Go stand over there. I'll take your picture." He pulled out his phone as I moved to the spot he'd indicated. I smiled as he snapped a few pictures, knowing my dad would love the fact that we stopped there.

"Wait." I moved to the spot where Elvis reached out his hand. I placed my left hand in it and raised my right arm in the air, mock-screaming like a crazed fan. I posed for an amused Caden who snapped a few more pictures.

"Now flash him," Caden called.

My face fell as I dropped my arms, glaring at his big dopey grin.

"It was worth a shot."

I rolled my eyes. "Your turn."

"I'm not really a fan."

I walked over to where he stood and grabbed his phone. "Yeah, but maybe there needs to be a picture to commemorate this brilliant road trip."

He smiled. I could tell he wanted to resist, but he hobbled over to the front of the statue on his crutches instead. I snapped a few pictures of him with his phone, admiring his easy smile as each picture froze on the screen.

"Hold on." I walked over and stood beside him, holding out his phone to take a selfie with Elvis looking down at us. Caden leaned his head in and we both smiled. "Say the King lives," I teased.

"Would you just take the picture?" he said with quiet laughter.

Caden

The girl ate like a fucking champ. The cheeseburger didn't stand a chance. Neither did the fries. She actually slapped my hand away when I tried to grab some. "You know, most girls wouldn't be caught dead eating a burger and fries."

"Then they're missing out," she said, popping a fry into her mouth.

I laughed, my eyes moving around the Elvis-themed diner we found down the block. It was Elvis overload with memorabilia filling every free spot on the wall. I glanced back to Finlay, happily eating across the table. "This wasn't exactly what I pictured when I pictured our first date."

"Date?" she asked with her mouth full.

I nodded. "I pictured something more—"

"Who said this was a date?"

I leaned back and crossed my arms, giving her a look at my impressive guns. "You're single and I'm single."

"That doesn't make it a date." Of course she challenged it. She had difficulty not having the last word.

"Well, why can't it be?"

She sat back and crossed her arms, clearly unimpressed and keeping us on a level playing field. "You didn't ask."

I smirked. "I'm Caden Brooks. I don't have to ask."

She cocked her head, her eyes leveling me with that unspoken sass I expected from her.

I resisted the urge to laugh as I glanced around at the Elvis fans filling the room. "Fine. Next time I'll ask."

Her eyes rolled so far into her head I thought they'd disappear.

"So…here's what I know," I said. "You like food, football, swimming, running, country music, and Elvis. What else is there to know?"

Her eyes lit up. "I'm not really an Elvis fan. My dad is. I stopped for him."

I tinge of jealousy tightened my gut. I couldn't imagine doing something like that for my dad. He'd never given me a reason to want to. My mom. Now that was a different story. I would've put my life on the line for her. "That didn't answer my question."

Finlay shrugged, her eyes drifting uncomfortably over my shoulder at something behind me. "That about sums it up."

"I don't believe that."

"Well, sorry to disappoint." She popped a couple more fries into her mouth, her eyes avoiding mine.

"You've never said where you're from."

Her brows inverted. "I haven't?"

I shook my head, wondering if that was her way of avoiding the question. "So?"

"Just a small town in Alabama."

"You always live there?"

She nodded, her eyes wandering out the window.

"You have any siblings?"

I watched her body tense as she swallowed down hard and shook her head.

"What'd you do the last two years besides try to find yourself?"

She looked back at me, a thoughtful expression in her eyes. "What do you think I did?"

"Backpack across Europe?"

She shook her head.

"Work at an island resort?"

She chuckled. "No."

"Join a circus?"

She tilted her head. "You suck at this."

I laughed. "Then just tell me."

Her eyes softened at the edges. "I worked in a place like this."

My eyes flashed around the gaudy diner. "Why?"

"Why what?"

"Why didn't you just go to college?"

I could see the worry lines in her forehead. Had I put her on the spot? Annoyed her?

She shrugged. "Just didn't." She finished off the rest of her fries without another word.

I grabbed for the salt shaker and teetered it on its side. I didn't like the quiet Finlay. I didn't like knowing I made her that way and had no idea why. "Now this's gonna sound lame—and normally I don't do lame, but what's your major?"

A small smile tipped her lips. "You're right. That sounded like a super lame pickup line."

"Would it have worked?"

"No."

"So?"

"So what?"

"What's your major, woman?"

She snickered. "Undecided."

"That's not a major."

"It's the best one I've got."

I stared across the table, wondering what someone like Finlay would want to do in the future. "I could see you as an ER nurse."

Her head shot back. "Really?"

I nodded. "The no-nonsense way you handle the guys. The way you're right there to assist on the field. The way you showed up and were willing to help me. You'd be a good nurse."

Her eyes lifted as she considered my words. "It's funny you say that because I always planned to do something in the medical field, then…" Her words tapered off.

I could feel myself inching forward, hanging on her words. "Then what?"

She shook her head, her eyes darkening. "Life just got in the way."

For some reason, I knew better than to pump her for more information. So instead I paid the check and we headed out.

An hour later, I watched her tired eyes in the rearview mirror. She was trying so hard to stay alert and focused. And away from a hotel. Alone. With me. I considered offering to drive, but the idea of us in the same bed again…let's just say thank God she couldn't read my mind. "Finlay. My phone shows a motel in eight miles. I want you to stop."

"We're only two hours from campus."

"Yeah. But I want to see Alabama again. In one piece."

Her shoulders dropped. It took a lot for her to admit defeat. That, or she was just terrified of being alone with me. Did she not trust me? Or was it herself she didn't trust? "Okay."

"Okay?"

"Don't sound so surprised. You've been making me think I'm exhausted for hours."

I laughed, knowing I totally had.

We pulled into the motel parking lot fifteen minutes later. Grass grew through the cracks in the pavement and the run-down building craved renovations. The odds of them having a gym or pool was nil. Finlay parked right in front of the entrance and opened her door.

"No. Let me." I grabbed my crutches and pushed open the door. "It was my idea."

She stared at me, looking so exhausted. I almost felt sorry for talking her into driving me in the first place. "Okay."

Once I stepped out into the warm night, it felt nice to put some light pressure on my leg. The doctor had assured me with rest, I'd be back on the field in no time. I just didn't expect it to be the truth given the severe pain and throbbing. But there I was, hobbling into the lobby of a seedy motel somewhere in Mississippi. A big orange cat sat on the counter and a foul musty stench nearly knocked me off my feet. I spun right back out the door. A night alone with Finlay was not going to be in a place like that. I opened the passenger front door and slid in. "It's a dump. You deserve better."

She stared at me, her skepticism mixed with exhaustion. "Why are you in the front seat?"

"I'm sick of looking at the back of your head."

She scoffed as the engine purred back to life. "I know. My profile is so much better."

"Why'd you do that?"

She gave me a sidelong glance. "Do what?"

"Put yourself down?"

"I just meant—"

"You're beautiful."

Her eyes rounded, her features fixed with fear. "What?"

"You heard me."

"Why would you say that?"

"Because it's the truth. And now I'm free to say it."

Finlay spent the next fifteen minutes silently staring straight ahead as we traveled through another unfamiliar town.

I wondered what she was thinking. I'd certainly given her something to think about. Now she just needed to figure out her feelings for me. Because I'd definitely been delivering mixed signals. It must've taken nerve for her to try to kiss me in the pool. But my reaction sucked. I was just so damn shocked, the only thing I could do was remember why I couldn't kiss her. Not that I didn't want to. It was all I thought about after she left me at the elevator. But it couldn't happen. Not when I had a girlfriend.

But even after putting herself out there like that—and being rejected, Finlay had still shown up at the hospital. And she'd stayed. No one made her. Those were both her decisions. And while driving me home was strongly urged, she'd still agreed. That had to mean something.

"Take the next exit." I pointed to a sign for lodging that appeared on the side of the road, hoping this place would be better. As tired as I was, I could see Finlay's eyes drooping by the minute.

She pulled off the exit and followed the signs until we sat in the parking lot of a reputable chain hotel. Its welcoming exterior and parking lot filled with cars told me this was the one.

"Maybe I can just close my eyes for an hour and then get us back on the road," she said.

"I forced you into this. The least I can do is get you a good night's sleep."

Clearly realizing it was a lot safer to sleep in a bed than drive on unfamiliar roads while exhausted, Finlay nodded.

I pushed open my door and stepped out, using my crutches for balance. "Be right back," I said before hobbling to the hotel entrance. I glanced over my shoulder. Finlay's eyes were closed and her head rested against the headrest. I smiled, knowing I'd gotten her to agree to not only spend the night with me, but to save me from hours in a car with my dad *and* any possibility of me becoming the man I hated most in this world.

CHAPTER THIRTEEN

Caden

Finlay stared at the king-sized bed in the center of the room. "They didn't have two beds?"

I shrugged as I brushed by her in the doorway. "It was this or the honeymoon suite. I figured this was better."

"You're lying."

"Yup." I dropped my bag on the chair and turned to her. "Aren't you coming in?"

"I feel like I've been set up."

"I've totally been planning to get hurt, end up in the hospital, and take a road trip with you for months."

She stared at me, her eyes clouded with embarrassment.

Shit. I hadn't meant to embarrass her. But knowing I had, I needed to make it better. "I can sleep in the chair if that makes you feel better."

She cocked her head.

"I'm serious. If you'd be more comfortable, I'm fine with it."

She walked inside, closing the door behind her. "I don't believe you."

I laughed. "Good. Because I'm so sleeping in this bed." I dropped onto it, kicking up my feet and grabbing the remote.

"I'm just gonna get cleaned up." Finlay moved into the bathroom with her backpack in her hand and closed the door behind her. She clearly needed some time to digest the precarious situation she found herself in, especially after I'd been pretty clear in laying my cards on the table—at least I hoped I had.

Once she locked herself in the bathroom, a familiar emptiness descended. I was getting so used to her being around, when she wasn't, it was as if a dark cloud had moved in. I pulled out my phone, needing to occupy my mind. I'd noticed in the car I already had a shitload of missed calls and undoubtedly angry voicemails from my father and Leslie. I doubted my father called Coach. That would've only shed light on the fact that I wanted nothing to do with him. But I hadn't listened to the messages or returned their calls. I didn't need that shit pulling me down when I was having such a good time getting to know Finlay.

The water in the shower switched on. The image of Finlay naked quickly made the thought of dealing with my father and Leslie a lot less irritating. So I went for it, listening to their messages, unfazed by my father's anger and Leslie's denial. Not about to call either of them back, I spent the next fifteen minutes watching sports highlights on TV.

Eventually, the shower switched off. My body hummed like a fifteen-year-old hoping to get laid for the first time. These were uncharted waters for Finlay and me. We'd never purposely shared a bed. We'd never been entirely alone with no chance of being disturbed.

A shuffling sound traveled through the bathroom door. I wondered what Finlay would do once she stepped out of the bathroom. Would she lay on the bed next to me like she had in the hospital? Would she lay on her stomach and watch television from the foot of the bed? Would she sit in the chair?

I didn't have to wait long to find out. The clicking of the bathroom lock pulled my attention from the television to Finlay stepping into the room. Her wet hair was in a messy knot on the top of her head and her short shorts and tank top clung to her body in all the right places. *Sweet Jesus.* She wasn't wearing a bra. Was she trying to kill me?

"How was the shower," I asked lamely, trying to keep my eyes from venturing to her chest.

"Good." She placed her bag down on the floor beside the chair and walked to the side of the bed. Without hesitating, she lay down beside me, fluffing the mound of pillows behind her head before looking to me. "Did your dad call?"

"Twice."

She scoffed. "You make a habit of pulling stunts like that with him?"

"Yup."

"Does it make you feel better?"

"Every damn time."

She laughed softly, and I wondered if she found my behavior to be immature or justified. She rolled onto her side, resting her head in her palm and looking at me, like really looking at me. "When does it end?"

Her question hit me hard in the chest. I'd never considered it before. I just knew I hated him and wanted him as far away from my mom and me as possible. "When I've had enough."

She nodded, and I wondered if my answer surprised her or stayed consistent with who she knew me to be.

"Leslie called too," I added, wanting to be honest with her.

"Oh. She must be worried about you."

I nodded. "Yeah. She doesn't believe it's over. She still thinks it's the meds talking."

Her brows lifted. "I didn't realize you broke up with *her*?"

I nodded.

Amusement danced in her eyes. "So she's not letting you break up with her?"

I rolled onto my side, my head resting in my palm. "It's not for her to decide." My eyes dropped to Finlay's lips, so pouty and pink.

"She's probably just sad." Realizing my focus was on her mouth, Finlay's words came out softer. "Are you?"

I shook my head, watching her swallow down hard. I liked that I made her nervous. Hell, she made me nervous. "I want to kiss you."

Her eyes jumped to mine, wide and nervous. "You do?"

I lifted my fingertips to her cheek, gently grazing them over her soft skin. She quivered under my touch. "Finlay, I haven't stopped thinking about you since you talked smack about my passes."

"What?" Her voice was hushed and incredulous.

My eyes remained fixed on hers. "And when you gave me shit for drinking too much water and cramping up, I wasn't sure if I wanted to strangle you or get you naked."

Her eyes rounded. "Why?"

"Why?" I looked her dead in the eyes so there was no confusion. "Because you're you. All spitfire and sass. All smart about football and life. And did I mention hot as hell?"

She smiled, almost sadly. "But what about Leslie? Isn't it too soon?"

My fingers brushed softly over her skin. As much as I hated the trepidation Finlay felt, she was right. I was being an insensitive prick trying to move on right after ending things with Leslie. Trying to get Finlay naked just solidified that fact. And while I should've been the rational one and put on the brakes, I'd learned in life nothing lasted forever. And right then, everything between us felt right. "I don't know what the hell I'm doing, Finlay. I just know I broke up with Leslie because I couldn't stop thinking about you."

Finlay shuddered as my thumb traced her jaw.

"I have no idea how I didn't kiss you in the pool when I wanted to. So. Damn. Bad." I rolled her onto her back, pinning her body to the bed beneath mine.

She pulled in a sharp breath as she gazed up into my eyes. "Your leg."

"I'm fine." I lowered my lips slowly, letting the anticipation build while I gauged her willingness to comply.

Her eyes drifted shut, her lips parting ever so slightly.

That was all the approval I needed. My lips sealed over hers. They were soft and inviting, just as I'd imagined they'd be. I sucked her bottom lip into my mouth. It was minty like she'd just brushed. I set the pace, eager yet steady. I tried not to get ahead of myself, knowing—whether I wanted to admit it or not—this had been a long time coming. But Finlay seemed more than willing to keep up. Her arms slipped around my back, her splayed hands holding me to her.

Encouraged by her fervor, I moved to her top lip, equally plump and sweet. She had no choice but to open for me. And when she did—when I knew she was all in—I devoured her mouth. No holds barred. This was pent up frustration coming to fruition. My tongue slid against hers. I couldn't get close enough. Neither could she. Her chest arched into mine as she pulled me closer. I wasn't the only one losing my mind. She was just as ready and willing. And the softness of her body beneath me was just about all I could handle. I wanted this. I wanted this with her.

I pulled back, my heavy breathing mirroring hers. She looked so willing beneath me. So ready for what I wanted to unleash on her. But I'd just broken it off with Leslie. What kind of dick would I be if I slept with Finlay? Granted I wanted to. But I wanted her to see everything between us was real, not some rebound thing. I squeezed my eyes tightly. *Fuuuuuck.*

"What's wrong?" she asked, her voice hushed.

I reluctantly opened my eyes, instantly met with Finlay's dazed gaze and flushed cheeks. Her chest rose and fell hard with each breath. Her shirt stretched tightly across her breasts, her pebbled nipples revealing just how into it she'd been. *Fuck. Fuck. Fuck.* She watched me, waiting for me to speak. "I think you're right."

She stared up at me with the same rejected look she'd given me in the pool. Only this time she was pinned beneath me with no way of escaping.

I cursed under my breath. "I promise you. This is one of the hardest things I've ever had to do. But I think I should probably just hold you tonight."

I watched the disbelief coast over her face. "Hold me?"

I bit down on my bottom lip to stop myself from taking back my words.

She blinked. "You're serious?"

I nodded, feeling my resolve waning. "Can I do that? Can I just hold you tonight?"

Her eyes held a mix of amazement and disappointment. And after a long torturous pause, she nodded. "Yeah. I'd like that."

I lay down beside her, wrapping her tiny body in my arms and pulling her front into my chest. "Trying to sleep is gonna be a lot harder now."

Finlay's laughter mixed with my own, somehow easing the awkwardness that existed now that I'd screeched on the brakes. "Yeah. I totally appreciate you being a gentleman and all, but maybe next time, give me some warning first."

I smiled, leaning down and pressing my lips to her forehead. "Next time, I won't be a gentleman."

Finlay

I could not freaking believe Caden was the one to stop us. I was all in. No matter how fast things were moving, I was ready and willing and throwing caution to the wind. But as I lay there in his arms, feeling so at home, I realized that rushing made no sense. If it was meant to happen, then we had plenty of time to explore each other that way.

"So do you know about all football or just Alabama?" Caden asked, his arms tightening slightly around me.

I shrugged. "Mostly Alabama." It was crazy how comfortable I felt with him with each passing minute. It was like, as soon as I decided to let him in, there was no longer anything stopping me. Not my past feelings for him. Not the notion that he'd had a girlfriend. Not my guilt for betraying Cole.

"How much do you know?" he asked.

"I don't know. Try me."

Caden's voice lowered to a sexy tenor as his fingertips skated up my back. "Oh, I intend to. Very soon."

A tremor moved through my already roused body.

"How many national titles do we have?" he asked.

"Sixteen."

He paused, likely considering a harder question. "How many number one draft picks have we had?"

I thought back to the trivia games my dad played with Cole. Some families played Candy Land. We played Alabama sports trivia. "One. Gilmer in the late forties."

He growled, annoyed with the depth of my knowledge. "Most famous player to come from Alabama?"

"Joe Namath."

"Wrong." He sounded pleased. "Julio Jones."

I tilted my head up so I could see his face. "You said famous. The guy was super famous and right behind Bart Starr for best QB."

"Yeah, but just think how great I'd look with Julio as one of my receivers."

I laughed, loving the connection we were forging in such a short period of time.

"How many Heisman winners have we had?" he asked.

"Two. Ingram and Henry. And coincidentally, they share the record for most rushing touchdowns—in case that was your next question."

Caden rolled me unexpectedly onto my back and covered me with his body. He grinned down at me. "You knowing all this stuff has me so horny, there's nothing left to do but get you naked or put a ring on your finger."

I laughed. "You're so stupid."

His smile faded, as if he suddenly remembered something. "Why'd Coach tell me to go easy on you?"

My eyes widened. "What?"

"When I called to tell him you were coming with me, he warned me to go easy on you and treat you right."

My chest tightened. My heart raced. Could I be honest with him? Could I talk about Cole? Could I drudge up something painful when I was feeling so happy? "I don't know." *Liar.* "He knows my parents. He was nice enough to offer me the job."

"Thank God he did," Caden said as he framed my cheeks with his big hands and dropped his lips to mine, having his way with my mouth once again.

There was no coming back from a night spent with Caden. Regardless of how innocent it turned out to be. My feelings were all over the map when it came to him. They couldn't be trusted. He made me feel things I'd never felt before. Things I wasn't sure I'd feel again. But that's why it was so scary. Because if he made my head feel so out of control, what would he do to my heart?

CHAPTER FOURTEEN

Finlay

"Do me a favor and don't become some crazy stalker," I warned Caden as he parked in front of my dorm, insisting on driving the final leg of our trip.

He turned to me with a grin. "Chances are I will. You have that effect on me."

"Well, just don't show up late at night looking to get busy."

He threw back his head and his laughter filled the rental car.

"I'm serious," I said with a straight face. "I may be entertaining another guy. Or worse, I have a roommate who'll not only stay for the action, but'll ask to join in."

The idea froze his features. "Are you kidding?"

My brows slanted. "She's got the no-filter thing you've got going on, so she'd definitely ask. But it's never happening."

He leaned toward me with quirked lips. "Well that's good. Because you're definitely all I can handle." He pressed his lips to mine, the kiss going straight to my knees. Even with students passing by on their way home from their Monday afternoon classes—the ones we missed, Caden had no intention of stopping, clutching my cheeks and holding me to him.

I could feel myself falling. Falling hard. And it scared the hell out of me. One of us had to stop before things got too intense right there for all to see. So I grabbed the door handle and pulled back from him, leaving us both dragging air into our lungs as if starved for it. "I've got to get inside."

"That's what I'm thinking," he said with a devilish grin that did crazy things to my insides.

"Can you turn anything I say into something dirty?"

He considered my question. "Is that a challenge or a question?"

I rolled my eyes, which just brought out a bigger smile. I wished I could smile too, but the thought that we'd be heading back to the real world made me uneasy. I didn't want to act like I expected anything from him now that our road trip had ended. I wouldn't be that girl. "So…I guess I'll see you at practice tomorrow." I tried to step out of the car, but he grabbed my wrist and pulled me back in.

He stared me down, looking more pissed than I'd seen him with Grady. "Yes, you'll see me at practice tomorrow. But you'll see me tonight because you're staying at my place."

The tenseness I'd felt just seconds before disappeared. "Is that a challenge or a question?"

He laughed. "That's me asking you to stay with me tonight."

I gazed into his eyes, feeling myself going over that cliff. That point of no return. "Is this moving too fast?"

"For who?"

I appreciated his attempt to ease my mind, but I still felt like it was happening too quickly.

"Finlay, the only people who matter are us. And do you care?"

I shook my head.

A smile slid across his face. "And I sure as fuck don't care."

I shook my head at his consummate honesty. "What time?"

He pulled in a deep breath. "I've gotta talk to Leslie first. I've gotta make it clear that it's over."

I nodded. And there it was. The sign that it was too quick. Sadly, I felt completely powerless because I liked how I felt around him. I liked how he opened up to me. I liked how we just fit.

"I'll call you once I talk to her."

I nodded again, stepping out of the car and opening the back door to grab my bag.

"Hey?" Caden looked over the front seat.

My eyes met his.

"Everything's gonna be fine. We're gonna be fine."

I smiled and for some reason, I believed him.

Caden

I hobbled up the front walkway of Leslie's sorority house. I'd tried her cell but my call went right to voicemail. I wasn't about to let her ignore me, especially after she'd called and left messages for me all night. A face-to-face sit down would put an end to it.

A rock held the front door ajar, so I pulled it open and stepped inside the front foyer like I had so many times before. This time I felt like an intruder. It wasn't my life anymore. I wasn't the sorority president's boyfriend. I wondered if the sisters knew that. Had she cried to them or maintained that we weren't actually over? Leslie was stubborn, and this was one fight she seemed dead set on winning.

I passed a few girls on my way down the carpeted hallway toward Leslie's corner room. They said hello, eyeing my crutches sadly. Did they pity me? Did they think my football career was over? I wanted to assure them I was fine, but why bother? Actions spoke louder than words. And me back on the field for our first home game would be proof enough.

I stopped in front of Leslie's closed door, sucking in a deep breath and hoping like hell this didn't go worse than our phone call. I tapped on the door and waited. Normally, I just walked inside, but I needed to draw a line. I needed her to see that wasn't our relationship anymore. I didn't want to be enemies, but I also didn't want to date her. I tapped again.

"She's not here."

I glanced over my shoulder at a girl who looked a lot like Leslie. Most of the girls in the sorority looked pretty similar to Leslie, all blonde, tall, and skinny.

"Where is she?"

"She went home. Said she had some personal stuff to deal with."

Part of me hurt for Leslie. What I'd done came out of left field. I was careless with her feelings, thinking I was doing the right thing. I didn't blame her for running to find solace in a place she felt safe. "She's not answering her cell. Could you let her know I stopped by?"

"Sure."

I turned on my crutches and made my way out of the sorority house. I had the urge to head back to Finlay's, but decided to get settled at home so I could try Leslie's cell again. She needed to know in no uncertain terms that it was over. She needed to know it wasn't her fault and she'd done nothing wrong. Feelings were a fickle thing and she was simply a victim of circumstance.

Finlay

"You're back," Sabrina squealed, greeting me at the door of our room.

I closed the door behind me, the scent of her vanilla lotion feeling like home. "Feels like I've been gone forever."

"You have. I missed you."

Unexpected warmth spread through me. No one other than my parents had ever said they missed me before. And it felt nice to be missed.

"I want to hear all about Arkansas. I saw Brooks' sack. Must've been awful up close."

I swallowed down a guilty lump. She had no idea what happened between Caden and me—no one did. But the way she said "up close" brought back a barrage of images from the hotel room. Images I wouldn't be shaking for a very long time. "I think it looked worse than it was." I walked over to my desk and dropped my bag onto the chair.

"Did you hear he and Leslie broke up?"

I spun around. "How'd you hear that?"

"She stopped by." Sabrina dropped down onto her bed. "She needed someone to vent to. Apparently there's someone else."

My forehead scrunched, my heart stuttering. "He told her that?"

Sabrina nodded. "She wanted me to ask you if anyone's been hanging around practices. Or if he's been with anyone on any of the road trips."

My eyes expanded. "How would I know?"

She shrugged. "You're around him. She thought maybe you've seen something."

I shook my head. "No." Even as the words left my lips, guilt consumed me. Guilt that I was lying to my roommate—my friend. And guilt that Leslie was hurt by Caden because of me.

Sabrina tilted her head, her eyes assessing my guilty face. "Finlay?" she asked hesitantly. "Are you the reason Caden broke up with Leslie?"

I gazed across the room at her, unsure what to say. I didn't want her to think differently of me because I was well aware it looked bad. But I wanted to be truthful. She'd been good to me. She deserved my honesty. "It just kind of happened."

Her eyes expanded. I braced myself for the backlash. For her to tell me I was a bitch. That she was ashamed of me. That she was disappointed in my poor judgment. But instead of anger or disappointment in her eyes, happiness brimmed as she jumped to her feet and rushed at me, nearly tackling me into a hug. "I'm so happy for you."

"You are?" My words were muffled by her shoulder.

"Are you kidding?" She pulled back, looking me in the eyes. "I could tell she wasn't hanging around me for me. I could tell she had other motives. Like she was milking me for information." She stepped back and crossed her arms. "So, Caden Brooks?"

I laughed. "I swear. It just happened."

"Uh, huh." She didn't believe me. Hell, I didn't believe me. Something had been happening between us for weeks.

"Have you kissed him yet?"

My eyes flashed away.

Her eyes nearly bugged out of her head, realization hitting her. "Did you do more than kiss him?"

I walked to my bed and dropped down onto it, purposely averting my gaze. "Let's just say, it came extremely close to going there."

"Don't you do that to me, Finlay Thatcher." She rushed to my side, dropping down on my bed beside me. "You can't say that and nothing else. I need this. I need to live vicariously through you on this one."

I clearly wasn't one to divulge my personal business readily, but the hopeful look in her eyes made it impossible to remain tight-lipped, especially given how excited she was for me. The images flooded my brain. His scent still clung to my clothes. My lips still tingled from his kiss. "He's an amazing kisser."

Her shoulders dropped. "So you're staying quiet? I respect that. But I can tell. Something happened. And whether or not you two got busy, something happened."

A full-blown laugh burst out of me as I fell onto my back. "I knew I wasn't the only one who said that."

She fell back beside me, both of us staring up at the ceiling. "I'm so happy for you. You deserve to have something amazing happen to you."

"Thanks." She couldn't possibly know the appreciation that small word held. She had become someone I trusted. Someone I was lucky to have in my life. Someone I could obviously depend on.

My phone pinged in my pocket. I pulled it out. The photo of Caden and me in front of Elvis filled the screen. The text beneath it read: **I miss my accomplice. Come over.**

A ripple rolled through my belly. I hadn't seen the picture of us together until that moment. We looked good together. The notion hit me fast and hard. He wanted me. Just me. In the photo I could almost see it. His eyes were soft, his smile was genuine, and the way he leaned into me was natural. Like that moment in time was how it was supposed to be. We looked happy. We were happy. And that notion felt so damn good.

"He's so hot," Sabrina said, looking at the picture. "Am I allowed to say that now that you two are a thing?"

I laughed. "You better. Don't want him losing that edge."

She laughed. "Why didn't he come in?"

"He needed to talk to Leslie."

Sabrina turned on her side, her head resting in her hand. "Good luck with that conversation. The girl's a pit bull."

I laughed. "Yeah. He said she wasn't letting him break up with her."

"Sounds about right."

We lay there for a long time. And for the first time in a very long time I felt content. Felt as though I'd found my place. Found people to rely on. Found something to look forward to each day. It had been a long time coming, but I actually saw a future with me happy. "Caden took Cole's position on the football team," I divulged.

"I didn't know that."

I shrugged. "You wouldn't. Caden doesn't even know."

"Are you planning to tell him?"

I nodded. "The time just hasn't seemed right."

"So, the jersey you have. That's Cole's?"

I nodded. "I've been working up the nerve to wear it down at the field. He only ever got to wear the practice jersey. Though the coach assured me he wore it around campus all the time."

Sabrina's lips slipped into a sad smile. "Sounds like someone I would've liked."

"Yeah. He was the guy you just wanted to be around." I blinked back tears, but for once it was okay. It felt good to talk about him. And cry about him.

"What happened, Finlay?"

I swallowed down the lump in my throat. "He had a heart condition we didn't know about. He collapsed on the field from sudden cardiac arrest. His heart just stopped with us hundreds of miles away."

She cupped her mouth with her hand. "Oh my God."

My eyes drifted toward my cork board and the pictures of him on it. "I guess looking back, it's right where he would've wanted it to happen."

"Doesn't make it any easier."

I shook my head. "Nope. It doesn't."

Caden

I sat on the porch in total darkness, my foot elevated on the small table in front of me. The rustling of footsteps through the fallen leaves Forester and I hadn't bothered to rake up drew my attention to the sidewalk. Finlay walked toward me, her fitted T-shirt, torn skinny jeans, and backpack already driving me wild from feet away. When it came to her, I was fucked. "Are you lost?" I asked.

A sweet, almost nervous, smile played across her face. "I don't think so."

"Maybe I wasn't clear. Are you lost without *me*?"

She laughed as she climbed the stairs, stepping onto the porch in front of me. "Your ego knows no limits, does it?"

"Nope."

She glanced down at my leg. "How's it feeling?"

"Better now that you're here."

She rolled her eyes as she dropped into the spot beside me on the porch bench.

I wrapped my arm around her shoulders and pulled her into me, dropping a kiss to the top of her head. "I missed you."

I could feel her body shake with quiet laughter. "It's only been a few hours."

"So?"

"How'd it go with Leslie?" she asked.

"I haven't talked to her yet. Apparently she went home. Told the sisters she had personal stuff to deal with."

"Does she think it won't be over if she runs away?"

I shrugged, though knowing Leslie, it was probably what she was doing. "I have no idea. She's not answering my calls."

Finlay's head lifted off my shoulder and her entire body turned to look at me. "I'm sorry she got hurt."

"Me too." I reached over and slipped my hand into hers, pulling her back into me. "I'm not someone who goes around hurting people. I feel like complete shit for what happened, especially the way it happened without warning. But my feelings for you were never innocent. I was just too scared to admit it, especially since I would've been breaking Leslie's heart on the off chance you'd feel the same way about me. I don't normally work that way. Dropping one girl for another. But to everyone else, including Leslie, that's how it's gonna look. Though I think we can agree, this didn't happen overnight."

Finlay nodded against me.

"I was wrong to stay with her. Had I broken it off sooner, it wouldn't have happened the way it did."

"Who said I would've been into you then?"

Who was she kidding? I stifled a grin as I pulled back and tilted my head to the side. "I can be pretty damn charming."

She arched her brows, a comeback brewing in her eyes. "You can be cocky."

"I've got a hell of an arm."

"You've got a hell of an ego."

"I'm hot," I countered with the smile I'd been told could melt the panties off any girl within a fifty-foot radius.

Finlay rolled her eyes. "You're maddening."

"And you love it."

Our laughter mixed in the quiet night as we continued to sit for a long time saying nothing at all. Being with Finlay was so natural. So comfortable. It was the way she put me at ease, but at the same time put me in my place with a mere look. I usually questioned people's motives. I wondered why they were around me. With Finlay, I didn't have to.

"You know what I think?" I said.

She shook her head.

"I think you need to see my room."

Her eyes narrowed on mine. "Seriously? Does that line work for you?"

"Stop worrying about what worked for me in the past. Is it working for me now?"

The sweet sound of her laughter carried through the darkness and right into my damn heart.

I pushed myself up and held out my hand. Finlay grabbed it and followed me inside. It took a little longer to make it up the stairs since I refused to use my crutches, but once we stood in the doorway of my bedroom, déjà vu washed over me.

This time Finlay didn't freeze in the doorway. This time she walked right into the room and dropped onto the foot of my bed, looking more at home than Leslie ever did in my space.

I lifted my brows, loving the sight of her there. "I think I'm gonna have to ask you again. Are you lost?"

She moved her head slowly from side to side. "Right where I want to be."

"Damn straight," I said, closing my door and stalking toward her. I reached behind my head and yanked off my shirt, tossing it to the floor. Finlay's eyes were fixed on my chest. I couldn't help the smirk that tilted my lips.

She didn't smile. She just lifted her hand and watched her own fingertips trail down my chest. My body quivered beneath her touch as she seemed to be memorizing every line and indentation. "God, you feel nice," she breathed.

I leaned down and she took the hint, scooting her ass back and laying down on my bed. I crawled over her, lowering my elbows on either side of her arms. "You think that felt nice? Just wait until I'm inside of you."

She dropped her head to the side to avoid my gaze, groaning at my honesty.

"What's wrong?" I laughed, lacing my fingers with hers beside her head.

"You're embarrassing me."

My forehead scrunched. "Why? I'm serious."

"Yeah, but..." Her voice trailed off.

I leveled her with my eyes, leaving no room for confusion. "I promise to be honest with you. Even if my honesty embarrasses you. It's not like you hold your tongue with me."

She chuckled softly.

"So when I say we'll take it slow, you can believe me." And though I smiled, I wondered how long I'd be able to hold off with her in my bed and on my mind. "It doesn't mean I won't spend the entire night touching you." I brushed my fingertips over her cheek, watching her eyes flutter shut. "Or kissing you." I lowered my lips and pressed them gently to hers, careful not to start anything I couldn't stop. I pulled back, moving to her ear and whispering, "Or telling you all the things I plan to do to you."

"You're not making this easy," Finlay groaned softly.

"Never promised to do that."

Finlay

Caden held my hand as we entered McMillan Hall the next morning. Sleeping beside him all night with his arms wrapped around me made it easy to forget there was a whole big world out there. But as soon as we stepped into the lecture hall, heads turned.

Why hadn't I considered people's reactions to Caden being with someone other than Leslie? Why hadn't I considered how they'd dissect me? I dropped Caden's hand. He glanced to me, disappointed. But he didn't grab for my hand. He let me trail beside him.

Most of the people we passed weren't focused on me. They were focused on their star quarterback who'd spent the night in the hospital after a crushing blow. They greeted him like the football god he was with big smiles and fist bumps, asking how he was feeling. Nothing about Caden's confidence faltered as he assured them they'd see him on Saturday. Since he'd opted not to use his crutches, they had no reason to doubt his words. And if Caden had his way, he *would* play on Saturday.

Bypassing his normal seat, Caden led me slowly up the steps toward my spot in the back of the room. I glanced to Leslie's empty seat. Thankfully she wasn't there to make a cringe-worthy scene. When we finally slipped into our seats, away from prying eyes, a rush of relief swept over me. Until I found Grady three seats over, his eyes assessing Caden and me.

"How ya doing, man?" he asked.

"All right," Caden mumbled without bothering to look at him.

Grady nodded, and I wondered if he understood the role he played in Caden's injury. Did he even realize it was his missed block that allowed Caden to get hurt?

My heart began to beat faster, and I wondered if round two of their locker room display would happen there in the lecture hall.

But Caden disregarded Grady's presence, pressing his lips to my ear instead. "Have I told you how hot you look in those cut-offs?"

I smiled as goosebumps rushed up my arms. "Like twenty times."

He chuckled. "I just wanted to be sure you understood." He slipped his hand back into mine, squeezing it gently. He clearly understood my discomfort with us flaunting our new status so soon after his break with Leslie.

At the end of class, Grady was smart enough to exit out the opposite side of the row.

Caden remained seated beside me. "I've got anatomy across campus," he said, stuffing his notebook into his backpack. "Where you headed?"

I tossed my bag onto my back and stood. "I've got an hour break before calculus."

"You done after that?" Caden asked.

"Yeah. Until practice."

He carefully pushed himself to his feet. "You wanna meet up for lunch?"

"Are you asking me out?"

His lopsided smirk slipped into place. "I guess I am."

"Well, for what it's worth. It's a lot better when you ask," I said, wondering if he understood my reference to our diner conversation.

He slipped his backpack onto his back. "Oh, yeah?" he said, draping his arm around my shoulders. "Then can we have sex tonight?"

I pulled away from him and shoved his shoulder.

"What?" he laughed. "You said it's better when I ask."

I shook my head as I moved out of our row. "You're so stupid."

"And you love it," he called from behind me.

* * *

I checked my phone as soon as I stepped into the hallway after calculus. There was no text from Caden, and I had no idea where to meet him. I clutched my phone as I made my way downstairs and out of the building. Once the fresh air hit, I stopped amid a rush of bodies moving in every direction. My eyes swept around the crowded area, stopping when I spotted him leaning up against a tree like he owned the place.

I took a minute to drink him in. His faded jeans riding low on his hips. His light blue shirt that matched his eyes and stretched across the muscles I had a front row seat to the previous night. The effortless way he commanded attention even in a crowd.

His eyes scanned the people moving all around, eventually landing on me. A smile spread across his face, stealing my breath away. If the rest of the world had just up and vanished, I would've never even known. My body nearly floated to him, his gaze an invisible lure. There wasn't a soul on campus who felt the elation I felt in that moment.

"Hey," I said, stopping once I reached him.

He said nothing, just tunneled his hand in the back of my hair and pulled me in for a kiss. A long breathtaking kiss that knocked me off kilter. When he finally pulled back, leaving me dazed and light-headed, he smiled down at me, absorbing the features of my face like he was trying to remember each and every one of them. "I missed you."

A flurry of butterflies swarmed in my belly. "I can see that."

He slipped his hand in mine and walked me along the path that bordered the quad. It was strange to think back to our first run-in on the same path. Sure, he still had a big ego. But there was so much more to him than just that. There was another side he didn't let everybody else see.

"Where we heading?" I asked.

"It's a surprise."

I stifled a smile. "I like surprises."

His eyes sliced to mine. "Good to know."

As we moved away from the bustling campus, Caden talked about his class and the cadaver he'd get to examine at the end of the semester. "If you apply to the nursing program, you'll have to take the class too."

"Oh. I can't wait."

He laughed at the fear in my voice before turning us away from the quad and weaving us through some administration buildings. We walked a little further until we came upon a group of trees behind one of the buildings. A bench sat in the shade of the trees' weeping branches. Caden stopped at the bench, guiding me down onto it. He pulled his backpack off his back as he dropped down beside me and pulled out a white paper bag. I knew that charbroiled smell as soon as he handed the wrapped sandwich to me. "For you."

I craned my neck to get a better look inside the bag. "There better be some fries in there."

He laughed, pulling out a big container of fries. "Only the best for you."

As I unwrapped my burger, I took in our pretty surroundings. You wouldn't even have known we were on a busy campus with all the trees and buildings concealing us. "What made you pick this spot?"

"Are you asking why we're all the way over here?"

I nodded as I bit into the burger.

"Just trying to keep you to myself."

I laughed, chewing down my bite. "Nice try."

He paused, staring out at nothing in particular. "I always felt like Leslie wanted people to see us together. Like she was showing me off—or at least staking her claim. You're not like that. And today when you dropped my hand, it was even clearer. We can come out here and you're gonna like it better than all the attention we'd get in the student union."

I blew out a long cleansing breath, blowing wisps of hair off my face as I did. "I'm so happy to hear you say that."

His eyes cut to mine. "Yeah?"

"I hated all the attention we got this morning."

His lips twisted regrettably. "I hate to say it, but you should probably get used to it. It's what comes with being my girlfriend."

My belly quivered at the word *girlfriend*. That single word having the ability to turn even the most sensible girl into a giddy teenager.

"And just so you know, you're not going anywhere."

"You're pretty confident." I feigned indifference, though I was shocked I managed to get a coherent sentence out after what he'd said.

"Oh, I'm confident. But I'm also not blind. And from where I'm sitting, what we've got going is pretty damn good."

I opened my mouth to respond, but he didn't give me a chance, swooping in and capturing my lips, kissing me senseless. He didn't bother letting go until he'd convinced me there wasn't a chance in hell I was going anywhere.

Caden

As soon as I stepped onto the field, my leg throbbed like a son of a bitch. Coach didn't want me pushing it, but I needed to show him he could count on me. I needed him to see I could bring us our first home game victory of the season.

"How's it feeling?" Coach asked as I stepped off the field after my third completion to Forester.

"Good," I lied.

"You think you can play Saturday?"

I nodded, knowing I could bear the pain if it meant putting another win on the board.

"I want you staying off it as much as you can. Ice it and elevate it at all times. And use the damn crutches."

"I'm no wuss, Coach."

His head recoiled. "Wuss? No. Idiot? Yes."

I chuckled to myself as he walked straight out onto the field, barking at one of the rookie receivers who dropped a routine catch. I sat down on the bench, taking the much-needed pressure off my leg for a couple minutes.

"Need a drink?" Finlay whispered from somewhere behind me.

I glanced over my shoulder. "Why are you whispering?"

She shrugged as she handed me a bottle.

"Well, stop it. And come sit with me."

She rounded the bench and slid down beside me.

I fought the urge to wrap my arm around her, knowing that would've embarrassed her. But I pressed my leg against hers to let her know I wanted to.

"How's your leg feel?"

I glanced around, ensuring no one was around before lowering my voice. "Honestly? It's hurting pretty bad."

"Caden, you—"

"I'm fine," I assured her, hearing the fear in her voice. "I'm gonna take a nice hot shower when I get home, then ice it."

"Oh, yeah?"

I studied the curious look on her face, wondering what was so interesting about me taking a shower and icing my leg. "Yeah, why?"

She worried her bottom lip. "Do you think you might need some help in there?"

My head retracted. "In the shower?"

Finlay stifled a smile and nodded.

Hot damn.

* * *

We fell through my front door kissing and grabbing at each other like we couldn't get close enough. Once we made it up the stairs and cleared my bedroom door, I slammed it and locked it behind me. I tore off my shirt and followed Finlay down onto my bed. Our mouths collided, our bodies desperate for each other. I pulled back, dragging in a breath and staring down at her flushed and panting beneath me. "I've seriously never had to hold off with someone I wanted to be with."

"Eww." She shoved at my chest. "Don't tell me—"

My lips crashed down on hers, shutting her up and stealing her breath away. I slid one hand down the side of her top, loving the feel of her shudder as my fingertips grazed the edge of her breast. When I reached the bottom, I slipped my hand underneath, slowly tracing the soft skin on her stomach as my lips continued devouring hers. My fingers itched to move upward, but I remained at her naval slowly circling it with my thumb.

She groaned into my mouth. The vibration traveling down to my balls, tightening them in a rush of need. I took it as my cue, trailing my fingertips up her ribs until I reached her bra. That wasn't going to cut it. I slipped my hand around, flicking the clasp in the back until her bra fell open. I circled my hand back around to the front, dragged my thumb over her nipple, feeling her quiver beneath me. I trailed it back down the same path, seeking a reaction. Finlay groaned into my mouth, the sensation reverberating in my chest. Unable to resist, I circled her nipple in slow circles until she writhed beneath me.

Fuck it.

I pulled back, peeling her shirt and bra up in one quick motion, clearing her head. Her unsteady breaths dragged into her lungs, her bare chest rising and falling in anticipation. I couldn't stop myself. I leaned down, taking her nipple into my mouth. Her back arched, her breast pushing closer to my face. I sucked it hard causing her to gasp. That just made me suck harder, earning me a desperate whimper. I tempered the sting with the soft swipe of my tongue.

Finlay hummed her approval as her hips bucked up. I knew what she needed. Knew what would bring that discomfort some relief. But I ignored her unspoken pleas, reaching for her other breast. I dragged the pad of my thumb over her nipple as her head pushed into the pillow and her back curved, somehow trying to get even closer. I trailed the same path back down and then circled slowly.

"Caden," she pleaded breathlessly.

"I've got you." I moved my mouth, sucking that nipple in.

Her back arched off the bed, her eyes undoubtedly rolling into the back of her head. "Oh, my God," she panted.

Relentlessly, I sucked and swirled my tongue around until I'd been tortured long enough by her body writhing beneath me. I lifted my head, considering my next move. Finlay's head shot off the pillow. She stared down at me, her eyes a silent plea—her body undoubtedly craving mine as much as mine craved hers. I reached for the button on her shorts and slipped it through the slot. Then tugged them with her underwear down her legs, tossing them to the floor.

Finlay naked on my bed was a sight to behold. If I could've held off any longer, I would've taken my time to admire the sexy view. Her dark hair spread out over the white pillowcase. Her perfect breasts. Smooth skin. Flat stomach. But I'd been patient. And my patience only stretched so far.

I shoved my shorts down my legs, careful not to bother my thigh as I rolled back on top of her. Instead of huffing at the weight of my body, she bent her knees and cradled me between them, like it's where she needed me. Hell. It's where I needed to be. "This is your last chance to back out. But let me tell you, you'll be leaving me cross-eyed and hard for days."

She grasped hold of my cheeks and stared up into my eyes. "I'm in." She pulled my mouth down to hers, this time controlling the kiss. Her tongue pushed inside. It was playful and eager as her hips moved beneath me, seeking relief from my erection.

I moved my knee, spreading her legs further apart and reaching my hand between them. She gasped as my fingers splayed her wetness, my thumb gliding back and forth between the lips until she trembled at the peak. I used the pad to circle and flick. She arched again on a moan. I couldn't stop. Seeing her aroused and beneath me. Hearing her quiet purr. It drove me fucking insane. I continued to circle and flick. Circle and flick. Circle and flick until her moans turned to growls.

"Caden," she pleaded against my mouth.

I couldn't hold off any longer. I reached for the drawer on my nightstand and yanked it open, digging inside and finding a small package. Thank fuck.

I pulled back and knelt between Finlay's legs, tearing it open and rolling the condom on while she watched my every move. I liked that she wasn't shy about my body. That she wanted to see every part of it. The feeling was mutual. I lowered myself back down, rocking my hips back and forth so the length of me trailed over her dampness.

"God, yes," she moaned.

I smiled. "You like that?"

She lifted her head. "Seriously?"

I chuckled, lowering my lips to the crook of her neck as I continued rocking my hips, letting her adjust so she was ready for me. She lifted her hips, aligning us. That's all the encouragement I needed. I latched onto her neck and I pushed inside. She groaned as her head dropped back, my weight stopping her from bucking me off the bed. I pulled out slowly, loving the slickness that made it easy to glide in and out, each time burying myself deeper. Soon, I hit my rhythm. Finlay seemed to like me slow and deep. So for as long as I could, I kept that pace, keeping us both at the brink.

"Are you trying to see how long you can do that without me losing my mind?" she asked.

I laughed. Not because it was funny, but because I could've done it all night long. But I wasn't the dumb jock some considered me to be. The desperation in her eyes told me what I needed to do. I reared off and continued my quest, this time faster. This time deeper. This time making sure to hit that spot right in front that was certain to make her see stars. And it did. Her body tensed, grabbing hold of me in pulsing successions that sent me damn close to the edge. I buried my face in her neck and thrust until my own body stilled, my release erupting out of me as she panted beneath me.

After a long moment of thanking God she gave in to me, I lifted my head. Finlay stared right back at me. "What are you looking at?" I asked.

"You." Her chest rose and fell with each hard-fought breath.

"And?"

"And you're pretty hot."

Laughter burst out of me as something tightened in my chest. It wasn't bad. It was terrifying. Because it was in that moment, as Finlay's green eyes gazed up at me, that I realized she had the power to destroy me in more ways than one. I knew it, and I was pretty damn sure she knew it too.

Finlay

I couldn't imagine waking up in Caden's arms would ever get old. I'd slept with my back to his bare chest all night, knowing I could've stayed like that forever. His scent enveloped me. His body centered me. And his grasp on me never once wavered. All of it was just too good to be true.

"Stop," Caden said, all raspy and sleepy.

"Stop what?"

"Thinking."

I turned in his arms. His eyes had barely even opened yet. "How do you know I'm thinking?"

"I know you."

"You think you know me."

He scoffed. "I know what you feel like when I'm inside you."

I dropped my face into his chest and groaned.

"What? Why does that embarrass you so much?"

Without lifting my head I shrugged.

"It shouldn't. Last night was amazing," he said, embarrassing me more than I thought possible. "So, you better not be regretting it. Because I'm not."

I lay there for a long time, not knowing what to say. The previous night surpassed my wildest expectations. The way he touched me. The way he whispered in my ear as his body moved with mine. The way he made sure every one of my needs was met before taking care of himself. He treated me right. But I couldn't shake the fact that I'd hated him for so long. I'd hated him when I didn't even know him.

I wanted to tell him about Cole. I wanted to ask him about the day of the wake. I wanted to clear the air once and for all. But the calm way his heartbeat drummed beneath my ear, as if he were at peace, was all too distracting. "How's your leg?"

Without warning, Caden rolled me onto my back. His sleepy eyes gazed down at me as his weight covered my body. "Good. But I could think of something that would make it feel even better."

I snickered. "Oh, yeah?"

He nodded, his lips lowering to my neck and trailing a path of glorious opened mouth kisses down it. "We never made it to the shower."

My eyes instinctively closed, the sensation causing my body to become languid. "We don't need to be to class yet."

His head pulled away from my neck. "Oh, yeah?"

I nodded as my eyes opened.

He kissed me hard then pulled back, just gazing down at me with the same soft look I was getting used to from him. The one that held possibilities. The one that made me feel special. The one I'd never imagined would ever be directed at me. "Stay tonight. And the next night. And the night after that."

I rolled my eyes. "I'm sure Forester would just love that."

"What? He's barely ever here. And, you wouldn't want me getting lonely would you?"

"You're pathetic."

He laughed before his eyes narrowed on mine for a long moment "This is crazy, isn't it?"

"What?"

"How right this feels."

My belly dipped as heat crept up my neck and into my cheeks. I didn't have sufficient words for how I felt. How hearing his words made me feel. But he didn't give me time to respond. He ripped the sheets off us sending a chill rushing over my naked body. Before I knew it, he threw me over his shoulder, laughing devilishly as he carried me into the shower with him. And he didn't release me until we were both late for our morning classes.

CHAPTER FIFTEEN

Caden

There was a knock on my front door the following night. Forester had disappeared as usual, so I just shouted from my spot on the sofa, where my leg was extended on the coffee table. "Come in." I hoped it was Finlay, but I knew she'd gone out for dinner with her roommate and planned to come by later.

Leslie appeared in the living room doorway, looking ready for a night out in a tight little shirt and short skirt that teased her ass cheeks.

My head instinctively shot back. "You're back?"

She smiled as she approached. "Hello to you too." She dropped onto the couch so her bare thigh pressed against my leg. "I missed you."

I sighed. "Leslie."

"Caden," she mimicked, teasing me like we were still together.

"This isn't a joke."

She dropped her hand to my thigh, moving it slowly up like she always did to get me hard. "Stop being so serious. We both said things we didn't mean."

I tried to inch away but the arm of the sofa stopped me. She knew she had me at a disadvantage, leaning in and pressing her lips to mine. My head retracted and my arms shot out, holding her at arm's length.

Her eyes flared as she jumped to her feet. "Why are you doing this to me? To us?"

"I tried being up front with you. I'd never cheat, and already I felt like I was. I shouldn't have been thinking about anyone but you, but it happened. So I ended it. It's only fair to both of us."

"No," she yelled. "It's only fair to you. You knew the only way to fuck some other girl was to get rid of me."

"That's not it. I told you. I didn't want to disrespect you. I wanted to do it the right way."

Her eyes narrowed in disgust. "There is no right way. I did everything for you, you selfish prick."

She wasn't going out without a fight. So I let her say what she needed to say. She was actually right. She had been there. She had helped me. And I was a selfish prick.

"Is the water girl going to do the same for you?"

I cocked my head. "What did you say?"

"Oh, don't think I don't know. I've heard you've been flaunting her all over campus. Besides, I saw the way you looked at her at your party. I'm not blind. Can't say I understand what you see in her. But I'm willing to overlook this little bump in the road. Especially now that I'm sure you'll want nothing to do with her."

"What's that supposed to mean?"

Leslie turned on her heels and walked to the entryway, returning with a jersey in her hand.

"What's that?"

A sly smirk tore across her lips. "Oh, wait for it. It's good." She opened up the number sixteen jersey, holding it up so I could read the name on the back: *Thatcher.*

It was as if the floor had dropped out from beneath me. The sight of that jersey—of that number and name—brought on a bout of sadness I hadn't allowed myself to feel in a long damn time. "Why do you have that?"

"Oh, this? It's not mine."

"What?"

She shrugged. "It's your water girl's. It was in her room."

My mind spun. Why would Finlay have Cole's jersey? I thought back to our trivia game. To all the things she knew about the history of the team. "She's a diehard Alabama fan," I explained, trying to convince both Leslie and myself that her love for the team was the real reason she had the jersey. Unfortunately, something told me it wasn't.

Leslie's smirk grew as she walked toward me. "Yeah. I bet she is." She extended her phone to me.

I grabbed it. "What?"

She nodded to the phone in my hand. "Just take a look."

The picture on the screen was a cork board filled with pictures of Cole and Finlay. And she wasn't in just one. She was in every damn one of them.

What the fuck?

"Apparently, the two of them dated," Leslie explained. "These were in her room, too."

A dagger plunging into my heart would've felt better than that news blindsiding me. Was Leslie right? Was it even possible? Had Finlay dated Cole?

My heart became a jackhammer in my chest.

How well did I even know Finlay?

Never once had she mentioned that she knew Cole. Never once had she mentioned anything about her past that I hadn't pulled out of her. Never once had I even considered our meeting had been anything but chance.

Jesus Christ.

"Seems like she's trying to dig her claws into every Alabama quarterback she can get her hands on. If you ask me, it's disgusting."

Fuuuuuck.

How could I have been so blind? So stupid? With Cole gone, had I been some kind of sick replacement for her? Had I just been another quarterback to warm her bed? Another star to latch onto to give her notoriety?

Heat pulsed throughout my body. I needed air. I needed a drink. I needed something to hit.

My mind whirled, flashes of our times together hitting me at warped speed. I'd let her in. I'd told her things I told no one. And all she was doing was using me. Worming her way into my life. And I'd fucking let her.

God dammit.

How could my feelings for her have developed so fast? Feelings so strong I'd broken things off with Leslie? It wasn't like Finlay had been easy to get close to. It wasn't like she hadn't made things difficult. But every move had been calculated. She'd played me like the fool I clearly was.

That shit stopped now.

Leslie lifted her shoulder. "Told you you'd want nothing to do with that football groupie."

The rest of Leslie's words were drowned out by the throbbing in my head. It wasn't the remnants of the hit that hospitalized me. It was the knowledge that I'd been used. *I'd been fucking used.*

I knew something wasn't right from the moment I met Finlay. But I chalked up her hot and cold attitude to her being overwhelmed by the guys and their antics. Once I got to know her, I saw her softer side. Her fun side. Her sexy side. But it had all just been a ploy to get to me. To insert herself into my life. To be part of my world. To benefit from my future.

Leslie was right. I didn't want anything to do with Finlay.

I'd never want anything to do with that lying bitch again.

CHAPTER SIXTEEN

Caden

Leslie had left hours ago, and I'd yet to move my ass off the sofa where I lay with the television muted and my head banging with the weight of what she'd revealed. I'd been fucking played.

Knocking on the front door jarred me from my thoughts. "It's open." I pushed myself upright as the door in the entryway creaked open.

Seconds later Finlay appeared in the living room doorway donning cut offs and a T-shirt. Her backpack was on her back, presumably filled with a change of clothes to stay the night. And despite what we'd shared, I felt nothing but disgust looking at her deceitful face. Remembering her traitorous touch. Inhaling her lying scent. I felt *nothing* for the girl who made me drop my walls and open up about my troubles with school and my hatred for my father. The one who made me break it off with a girl who dedicated her time to helping me. And loving me.

Everything about Finlay was a fucking lie and I fell for it. Hook. Line. And sinker.

"Hi." She smiled. Of course she smiled. She'd bagged the quarterback. She got him to dump his girlfriend. She pulled the wool right over his eyes.

I did nothing but stare at her. At a girl I'd never known. How had I been fooled so thoroughly? How had I been so damn stupid?

"Are you okay?" she asked as she stepped into the room, slowly approaching the sofa.

I shook my head. "Nothing about this fucked up situation is okay."

She sat down next to me, dropping her backpack onto the floor at her feet. I moved a couple inches away, not wanting to touch any part of her. Her eyes took in the distance. "You want to talk about it?"

"Talk about what?"

Her eyes narrowed, caught off guard by the cold clip to my voice. "Whatever's going on."

"Leslie stopped over."

"Oh. How'd it go?"

"You mean, me breaking up with the one girl who had my best interest in mind?"

Finlay's brows drew in.

"The girl who took classes with me to make sure I passed. The girl who cared about my future?"

Finlay's head recoiled, clearly taken aback by my escalating anger.

"The girl who always told me the *truth*."

"What am I missing?"

I grabbed the number sixteen jersey from the floor beside the sofa and pulled it tightly to show *Thatcher* on the back.

Finlay's eyes shot wide, the fear immediately evident. "Where'd you get that?"

"So, it is yours?" I guess a part of me held out hope that it wasn't.

"Did Leslie bring it over?" Her voice hardened. "She stopped over to see my roommate. She must've taken it."

"So you're not even gonna deny it?"

Her eyes cast down as she shook her head.

"So, what? You just thought I wouldn't find out?"

"I wanted to tell you."

"It's a little late, isn't it?"

Her eyes flashed up. "At least you know now."

"Are you fucking kidding me?" My voice grew louder, angrier. Her body instinctively inched away from me. "I had to find out from the girl whose heart I was breaking for you. *You*. Someone who wasn't even honest with me."

"What are you saying?"

"I'm saying you're a liar."

Her sharp intake of breath was hard to miss. "I'm a liar because I left out something I didn't feel comfortable bringing up?"

"You didn't feel *comfortable* bringing it up?" Rage radiated off me. Every part of me shook.

"My father was a liar. I've had enough of that shit in my life. I don't need it from you, too."

Her face was incredulous, like she couldn't fathom why I was so angry. "So that's it? I'm a liar? What now? You're gonna stay with Leslie?"

"At least I can trust her."

A scary smile slipped across Finlay's face. "Well, I've gotta hand it to you, Caden. Real clever. Taking a break from Leslie so you could sleep with me with no repercussions. Genius." She shook her head as she stood from the sofa. It was her turn to look disgusted.

"I'm sorry you feel like I wasn't honest with you. But right now, you're the one who's not being honest with yourself."

After what she'd done, she wasn't going to call me a liar in my own house. I lifted my chin toward the door. "The door's over there."

She tried to stifle her gasp as she leaned down to grab her backpack, but I heard it. She stood back up with her chin tipped defiantly.

"I'm gonna pretend this never happened," I said, wanting to be clear that we were done.

Finlay's eyes narrowed, searching my face like she'd never seen me before. Like she didn't know me. "Fuck you." She turned toward the door and stormed out of my house and out of my life.

CHAPTER SEVENTEEN

Finlay

Every part of my body shook as I attempted to fill bottles at the locker room sink. Not only was I still vivid and stunned by Caden's unceremonious blow-off the previous night, but I was also embarrassed. People had seen us together. People had seen how happy I must've looked by his side. Now I had to face everyone. Face them knowing I'd been stupid to believe he actually cared about me. I must've been the laughing stock of campus.

Grady had warned me that Caden wasn't Prince Charming. I never thought I'd agree with anything Grady said. Yet there I was, wishing I'd heeded his warning. Wishing I'd listened to my own feelings about Caden.

"Water girl."

My eyes cut over my shoulder. Forester, Caden's roommate, held out his hand for a bottle. The guy was gorgeous. If I didn't hate his roommate so much, I may have smiled at him and all his confidence. Instead I just tossed him the bottle and turned away.

"I need another one for Brooks," he called.

I spun back around shooting him daggers. "He can't get his own?"

Forester shrugged. Something about him acting like he didn't know what happened made me even more pissed. I threw him the bottle a lot harder than I should have. But since he was used to catching passes over his head from sixty yards away, he didn't even blink as he nabbed it.

Maybe he didn't. Maybe I was such an insignificant encounter that Caden didn't even bother mentioning it to his roommate.

Halfway through practice, Coach motioned me onto the field to bring the players water. Caden didn't even look up from his squatting position in the center of the huddle as the other guys stuck out their hands for a bottle. His leg didn't seem to be giving him any trouble out there. I wondered if he was just sucking up the pain so he could play.

As angry as I was, I still couldn't understand why Cole being my brother was such a deception to him. Didn't he realize talking about my brother was difficult for me? Didn't he know I didn't hide it to hurt him? I knew football players took bro codes seriously, never dating their teammates' sisters. But to despise me so much because of it…it just didn't add up.

I'd wanted to believe he wasn't the guy I initially believed him to be. I'd actually convinced myself he wasn't. But I should've gone with my gut. Because in the end, I'd gone against my better judgment. I'd given him the chance he didn't deserve. And for what? To be cast aside because I hadn't been up front about Cole.

Screw him.

If anyone had the right to be angry, it was me.

* * *

"Quarterback at three o'clock," Sabrina said, staring with wide eyes over my shoulder.

"You do realize I saw him at practice, right?" I glanced over my shoulder across the student union where we were grabbing a quick dinner. Caden sat with Forester at a table, drawing the normal attention football players garnered in crowded places. Usually it was their size and loud mouths that drew the attention, but Caden and Forester in one place was more than most girls could handle.

Stupid girls.

"What did he say?"

I stuffed a fry into my mouth as I looked back to Sabrina. "Nothing. Acted like I didn't exist."

"Ugh," she groaned. "What's wrong with him? He should be groveling. He should be begging you to—" Her words stopped as her eyes locked on something else behind me.

I followed her gaze. My stomach lurched as Leslie stopped at Caden's table. If love was a strong emotion, hate was stronger. And I was good at hating. I'd hated Caden for two years. It came easily. And I could say with much certainty that I hated Leslie. It didn't faze her that Caden didn't want her. She just knew she'd been scorned and didn't care who else got hurt.

Don't get me wrong. He wasn't blameless. Everything he told me about why he broke up with her could've been a ruse to get me in his bed. Maybe he really did want her and not me all along.

Leslie nodded, then walked away from his table. I guess the happy couple hadn't been reunited after all. But it was as if she knew I was watching because her big blue eyes shot over her shoulder, latching onto mine. Her lips pulled up in one corner, like she wanted me to know she'd torn us apart.

I held her stare. I wasn't one for revenge, but looking at her gloat across the crowded room made me want to tear her extensions out and wrap them around her skinny little neck.

"I dropped out of my pledge class."

My head whipped back to Sabrina. "What?"

"After what she pulled, I don't want to be friends with people who'd use me to hurt my friend."

I stared across the table at this girl who had my back, thanking anyone who was listening for putting us together. "I'm sorry. I know how excited you were."

She shrugged. "Eh. I'll live. Most of the girls had sticks up their asses anyway."

I laughed, remembering Caden's phone call with Leslie. I glanced back over at him. He could care less I was in the room as he laughed and carried on a conversation with Forester.

Turned out I had been nothing more than a mere detour for him.

* * *

If I can't have him, neither can you.

The text came as I lay on my bed studying for my psychology midterm. There was no question who it came from. At first I wondered if Caden had given Leslie my number to harass me. Then I remembered he'd used my phone to call her the day of his party. I contemplated ignoring her text. Contemplated firing back. But did I really want to stoop to her level?

Stay away from him, bitch.

I pulled in a sharp breath as my fingers pounded away at the screen. **Nope. I work for his team.**

I barely blinked before another text appeared. **Quit.**

A humorless laugh burned the back of my throat. Who did she think she was?

Another text popped up. **And so you know, Caden and I WILL be back together.**

I rolled my eyes and responded. **Then I shouldn't be a problem, should I?**

I stared at the screen, waiting for the three dots indicating she was typing to appear. They didn't. I wasn't sure if I'd shut her up or just pissed her off.

Time would tell. It always did.

***

I arrived at the lecture hall early for my psychology exam. Sure, I'd been distracted by what turned out to be a shitty week, but plugged away nonetheless and studied until I knew the information. I glanced to Grady's empty seat, wondering if he even realized we had a midterm. Probably not.

My eyes strayed toward the section Caden sat in earlier in the semester. Neither he nor Leslie had shown up yet. A jealous knot twisted my insides, unprepared for them to show up together. There were just some things I didn't need to see.

I buried my nose in my book, rereading the chapter on chromosomes. Rustling to my right nabbed my attention. Grady sat there, having entered from the other end of the row. He eyed me, before venturing a glance at the empty seat beside me.

I lifted my shoulder, my only response to his unspoken observation. He'd warned me about Caden. I was just too stupid to listen.

Surprisingly, he didn't gloat. Instead he shuffled through the stack of disheveled papers sticking out of his notebook.

As my eyes moved away from him, I noticed Leslie had arrived, all decked out and staring at the entrance from her normal seat. Within seconds, Caden strolled into the room. His confidence never ceased to amaze me. I couldn't tear my eyes away from him, needing to know what he'd do. Needing to see it with my own two eyes.

And then, as if it were a slow-motion movie sequence, Caden didn't even glance at Leslie who stared him down, waiting for him to sit with her—or at least acknowledge her. He did neither. Instead, he walked across the front of the room and slipped into a seat in the first row of the middle section, a good twenty rows in front of me.

A small sense of relief fell over me. As much as Leslie fought to hold onto him, he had other plans—plans that didn't include her or me for that matter. But at least she didn't win.

No one did.

* * *

Saturday's first home game brought Alabama fans out in droves. The stadium, filled with over a hundred thousand people, was a sea of crimson. The noise level was off the charts and excitement filled the air. My parents made the trip, not wanting to miss the first home game, especially now that their daughter was part of the team. I knew it would be difficult for them. It was the first game they'd attended since losing Cole. That's why I invited Sabrina along. She'd definitely make their experience memorable.

I glanced over my shoulder, spotting them sitting in the section behind the bench where the tickets I'd given them were located. My mom's head was thrown back as she laughed at something Sabrina said. My dad's eyes were on the field, watching the guys warm up. I could see the sadness in his eyes as he watched Caden toss the ball around with his backup. I understood my dad's sadness. I felt it every time the players ran onto the field. It always felt wrong to me. Like I knew Cole was supposed to be there.

My dad's eyes flitted over to mine and a huge smile lit up his face. I waved at the same moment he lifted his hand to wave to me. My mom must've noticed because she started waving. Then Sabrina joined in. I laughed from my spot on the sideline, feeling encouraged by their presence there.

"Hey."

I spun around, my face falling as Caden walked toward me. It was the first time we'd even looked at each other since I was kicked out of his house. I'd been avoiding him, and he'd been avoiding me just as much.

"I need a drink."

Oh, hell no. He may have ordered me around in his house, but not here. Not in a place I was just as welcome as he was. "You know where it is."

His eyes narrowed coldly, like he was looking at someone he despised.

"I assure you, the feeling's mutual," I said, trying to keep my composure with the stadium filled with people, and the eyes of many likely on their star quarterback.

He said nothing, just walked over to the table and grabbed his own bottle before walking away.

Yvette, who'd been sitting on the bench, approached me. She leaned in toward my ear, needing to speak up for me to hear over the noise. "He's got it bad for you."

I scoffed. The girl clearly had no clue.

She nodded. "I've seen the way he's been looking at you all season. And now, when something's clearly up between the two of you, he's always looking when you're not. He's got it bad."

"Well, he's got a screwed-up way of showing it."

She shrugged as she turned back to the bench, walking into the bodies lining the sideline.

I looked out at Caden on the field, wishing more than anything it was Cole out there. Someone who breathed Bama. Someone who had the heart of a lion and not of a coward. Someone who treated everyone with respect. Someone who deserved that spot.

* * *

"I was so proud of you out there," my dad said, beaming from across the table in the quiet off-campus restaurant.

I rolled my eyes at Sabrina beside me before looking to my dad. "I hand out water."

"And you do it like no one I've ever seen before," he assured me.

My attention moved to my mom beside him. "Has he been hitting the bottle again?"

She laughed as she reached across the table and placed her hand over mine. The gesture feeling like home. "He's just happy to see you out on the field. It's always been his dream to have a child out there." Her smile faded as she lifted her hand from mine and wiped the corner of her eye to stop a tear from trickling out.

I nodded. "I know."

"So, how are the guys treating you?" my dad asked, trying to lighten the suddenly somber mood.

I shrugged, my eyes drifting out the window. The moon shone big and bright over the parking lot speckled with cars.

"Grady's a jerk," Sabrina said, jumping into the conversation like she'd known my parents forever.

"The right tackle?" my dad asked.

I nodded, glancing back. "Yeah, but since I made him think I spiked his water with a laxative, he leaves me alone."

They all laughed, apparently not realizing I'd been serious.

"If anyone can handle a bunch of jocks, it's you," my mom added, knowing what a little tomboy I'd been growing up.

"There's also Caden Brooks," Sabrina offered.

My eyes cut to hers.

"What?" she asked all innocently. "They should know you two had a thing and now he's being an ass."

"You and Caden Brooks?" My mom's astonishment was understandable. She knew my feelings toward him. Knew how much I despised the very ground he walked on.

I shook my head. "It was nothing. We thought there might be something there, but it wasn't right."

My parents exchanged a look of sadness, but they did what I knew they'd do. They let me make my own choices. My own mistakes. They weren't the type of parents who pried—or lectured. They felt the lesson I learned, and the heartbreaks I endured, just made me stronger.

I just wished it was the truth.

CHAPTER EIGHTEEN

Finlay

A week of awkward practices ensued where I avoided Caden and he avoided me just as much. If I walked into the locker room when he was alone, I turned and walked back out. He did the same. It was an unspoken agreement that we both gladly adhered to.

When I climbed the bus for our game in Mississippi that Friday, Yvette had yet to arrive. I took my aisle seat, busying myself with my phone so I didn't have to face Caden. There was already a text from Leslie awaiting me.

I have eyes everywhere.

I shook my head. The girl was psychotic. **You should probably contact a doctor about that.**

Her response came immediately. **Stay away from him.**

Her fear of me was way too amusing not to respond. **For someone so confident, you sure do worry a lot about me.**

Don't mess with me, bitch.

Oh, no she did not. My fingers flew across the screen. **I assure you, your ex is a lot more fun to mess around with.** I couldn't contain my smug grin imagining Leslie fuming at the thought of Caden and me far from home at another hotel. I didn't even bother waiting for her response. I shut down my phone and tucked it into the bag at my feet.

When I sat up, Caden made his way down the aisle. I contemplated telling him to keep his ex on a tighter leash, but decided I'd be giving her too much power to even mention it. It didn't matter, though. He walked right by me, shifting his hip to avoid touching any part of me as he passed by.

For the first time in over a week, his snub sent a cold chill up my spine. And as much as I hated to admit it, it was the realization that I was completely alone there. Alone on a crowded bus. Caden had been my only friend on these trips, even when I hadn't realized it. Whether he sat beside me on the bus or met me in the gym or pool, I could always count on those conversations. Now, I had no one to talk to. And that sucked.

After practice at the stadium, I stayed in the hotel room while the team went out for dinner for obvious reasons. Having the room to myself, I'd watched a movie then fallen asleep way too early. By three in the morning, I was wide awake. No way in hell I wanted to risk running into Caden, so I avoided the pool and gym, opting to jog outside instead.

I made it to the entrance of the hotel, stopping when I stood in darkness outside the front overhang, rethinking my grand plan.

"Hey."

My body stiffened.

Forester materialized out of the darkness from the direction of the parking lot. "Where're you going?"

I shrugged. "Thought I'd go for a run."

His ice blue eyes focused on mine. "No swimming tonight?"

My forehead scrunched. If he knew Caden and I met up, how much more did he know? "Not tonight."

He buried his hands in his pockets, standing awkwardly across from me for a long moment. He sure was stunning up close and out of uniform. "Listen, I have no clue what happened between you and Brooks cuz guys don't bitch to each other the way girls do. But I can tell you this. The way my boy's been walking around pissed at the world is a big difference from the way he used to look when he was sneaking out for a swim."

I shrugged. "Yeah, well, your boy has a way of not hearing people out."

He held up his palms, seemingly amused by my tone, which come out harsher than I intended. "Hey. It was just an observation. I wasn't prying."

"Sorry," I mumbled.

"For what it's worth, guys think with one thing and one thing only. So if that's all he was thinking with, he wouldn't be this bummed."

I nodded, appreciating him trying to make me feel better. Because in reality, we didn't know each other. "Where are you coming from?"

The coolest smirk I'd ever seen swept across his perfect lips, and a dimple dug into his cheek. "Had someone to see."

I raised my brows.

He snickered. "Why don't you run in the gym," he suggested. "I'd feel a lot better knowing you weren't running around some unfamiliar town in the middle of the night."

My eyes cast down, embarrassed he felt the need to take care of me. Was I really that pathetic?

"I'll make sure Brooks stays in our room," he assured me.

My eyes lifted, appreciating his assistance more than I realized. "Thanks."

He nodded, before turning and disappearing into the hotel.

* * *

Monday morning I hurried out of the fine arts building, feeling exhausted from the weekend road trip. I must've been more dazed than I realized because I slammed into the person walking into the building at the same time. I shuffled back a few steps, completely jarred by the collision.

"Watch it," a familiar voice warned.

My eyes shot up. Leslie glared at me as she readjusted the fallen strap on her bag. My eyes narrowed. "Why don't *you* watch it? And while you're at it, stop texting me."

An insincere smile pulled at her lips. "You know," she said, eyeing the people moving around us, "I actually feel sorry for you."

A humorless laugh shot from my throat. "Oh, I've just got to hear this."

"You had a professional football prospect within your grasp and you couldn't hold onto him."

No matter how I felt about Caden, my stomach still roiled at her words. "A professional football prospect?" I blinked hard. "Is that really what you see when you see him?"

"Don't try to make this something it's not," she snarled.

"You're doing a fine job of that all on your own," I laughed, actually amused by her.

"Shut up."

I smiled. "Why? Because now you realize the first thing that came to your mind was his future career?"

"Oh, and it's not what you were thinking when you were trying to worm your way into his life?"

"Nope. It wasn't." I shook my head. "I actually feel sorry for you. Planning your life in some big house with a guy you want for all the wrong reasons. Do you even realize how smart he is? How thoughtful he can be when he's not being brainwashed by people like you? How his past shaped him into the loyal person he is? Or have you missed that while you were counting your cash—I mean *his* cash?"

"That's not how it is," she scowled.

"Then how is it, Leslie?" Caden asked from behind us.

My body tensed at the sound of his voice. I spun around, expecting him to be glaring at both of us, but his eyes were locked on Leslie's.

"You know that's not what I meant," she said with the brush of her hand.

He shook his head. "No. I don't."

I turned from the scene, moving away quickly. If he'd heard Leslie, then he'd heard me. And there was no way I wanted to face him after I'd actually stuck up for him.

But damn it felt good to put Leslie in her place.

"Finlay, wait!" Caden called from behind me.

I quickened my pace, weaving my way through people hurrying to their classes, blending amongst them, and trying to forget about the entire scene.

I ate my lunch alone under a secluded tree—far from the trees Caden had taken me to. But by ten to three, I'd stalled long enough and needed to get to the field for practice. I passed a few of the guys on my way into the field house, keeping my head down so not to run into the one I didn't want to see.

"Finlay!" I could hear Caden's feet slapping on the tile hallway as he jogged after me.

I quickened my pace and walked right into the locker room.

"Just stop for one second," he said as he entered the locker room behind me.

I stopped and spun around with my teeth clenched. "What?"

The players getting suited up stopped, their attention moving to us.

"Talk to me."

The run-in with Leslie and the way he all of a sudden wanted to speak to me after almost two weeks of radio silence pissed me off. I stormed back toward him, stopping only when the tips of my toes touched his. "Why? Because Leslie showed her true colors? I don't think so." I turned around and started to walk away.

He caught my arm. "Wait."

I yanked my arm free as I spun back toward him. "You made up your mind about what happened," I said, trying to keep my voice down and my escalating anger in check. "Why do we need to talk about it?"

He shoved his hands into his pockets. "I just felt blind-sided."

My brows shot up. "Blind-sided?"

"That you dated Cole."

My face fell, my mind spinning with his words—his inaccurate and completely crazy words. "Who told you that?"

"Finlay," he sighed. "You have his jersey and his pictures plastered all over your room."

The air punched out of my lungs. That's what he thought I lied about? That's why he ended things?

"I deserve to be pissed you didn't tell me." His voice cut through my shock. "It all just seemed too convenient you'd now want to be with me."

My shock morphed to disgust. "*You* deserve to be pissed? So let me get this straight. Your ex goes through *my* stuff. And she didn't just go through it, she *took* it. But I'm the wrong one here?"

His eyes cast down.

"Then she runs to you in hopes of what? You'd think I'm some lying quarterback groupie? Oh, wait. That's exactly what you think."

"I have no reason not to."

Audible winces from the guys in the locker room reminded me we weren't alone. But their responses only reinforced what I already knew. Caden was wrong. He'd been wrong all along. And he chose to believe a lying bitch over me. How could he not see the truth when it was staring him right in the face? "Screw you."

His eyes narrowed. "Why? Because I found out the truth?"

Another round of winces spread around the locker room.

I wondered if any of the guys knew Cole was my brother or if they just thought Caden was a total idiot. I harnessed every last bit of restraint I had. "If that's what you really think of me, then you don't know me at all." He reached for my arm, but I yanked it away. "Don't."

"Who's ready to go kick some ass out there?" Grady shouted as he barreled into the locker room, pulling the unwanted attention from us.

I glared at Caden. "Stay away from me." I shook my head, disgusted and spent. "You are exactly what I thought you were." With that I turned and stormed into the back room to do my job. The real reason I was there.

Caden

"Dude. You seriously fucked that one up," Grady's voice taunted me from behind.

I spun around, ready to throw down. "What'd you say?"

He lifted his chin toward the door Finlay disappeared behind. "The girl knows football. Puts football players in their place like it's no big feat. Can drink Miller under the table. And she likes your sorry ass. How do you go and blow something like that?"

My teeth clenched, the tick in my jaw pulsing. "Says the guy who won't stop busting her balls."

"Dude. You always tease the ones you like. And she's cool shit. I just knew she needed to toughen up. Didn't want the guys eating her alive."

I shook my head at his ridiculous rationale.

"So what'd she do?" he asked, leaning down and unzipping his bag on the floor in front of his locker.

I glanced around the suddenly empty room. The guys had fled, clearly worried we were gonna go at it again. I looked back at Grady's ugly mug. Did I really want to be having this conversation with him? "She lied."

"Who doesn't?" He reached into his bag. "Did she cheat?"

"No."

He glanced up. "Sell your shit online?"

I shook my head.

He pulled out his practice gear. "Talk to the tabloids about you?"

I shook my head.

He shrugged. "Then from where I'm standing, you need to fix that shit before she's warming some other dude's bed."

Knots of unease formed in the deep recesses of my gut. Was Grady right? Had I lost the best thing that ever happened to me? I thought back to the scene earlier. Even though she hated me, she still stood up for me with Leslie. She didn't have to. If I'd really just been a replacement for Cole, why would she bother?

Finlay

My eyes scanned the packed bar where Sabrina and I had been drinking for hours at a corner table. She claimed our fake ID's needed breaking in and *I* needed a girl's night out like no one's business. And though I was hesitant at first, being out helped.

After the run in with both Leslie and Caden, I needed to forget everything. I needed to let loose. I needed to move on. Sabrina was great at helping me make that happen. More than once she'd wrangled in some hot guys to buy us drinks. None of them were great at conversation, but it didn't matter. It was just nice having attention from guys who didn't hate me.

"I still can't understand why he hasn't apologized," Sabrina said over the loud music.

I took a long swig of my beer. "He still thinks I'm a liar." *Oh, shit.* I could hear the slur in my voice and that never ended well. "He thinks I dated Cole and now I'm after him because I have this thing for quarterbacks." And I was getting loud. Fan-freaking-tastic.

Her brows met in the middle. "You didn't correct him?"

"He judged me before hearing the truth." I lifted my beer to my mouth and took another long swallow. "He doesn't deserve it now."

Sabrina picked at the label on her bottle. I could see in her way-too-focused-eyes that whatever came next would be a doozy. "Finlay. Sometimes there's more to the story than meets the eye."

I cocked my head, wondering why she hadn't immediately agreed with me. "I let him in, Sabrina, even when I knew I shouldn't. Then he didn't give me the chance to explain because, oh that's right, he was too busy kicking me out of his house."

"I've got your back, you know that, right?"

I nodded.

"So just think about it from his perspective. Do you blame him for thinking you dated Cole? It does kind of look that way."

My eyes flashed away, unsure how to respond. I was the one who'd been hurt. I was the rational one. Caden was the irrational one. He was the one who'd hurt me. He was also the one walking into the bar with Forester at that very moment. *Shit.* "We need to leave."

"What?" Sabrina's head whipped in the direction of my eyes. "Oh, I think we're staying. This is about to get good."

I shook my head. "Nope. Me, too much beer, and him in the same place have bad written all over it."

Sabrina laughed. "I think you two have some talking to do."

"I'm serious. I'll talk to him. Just not here. Not with me like this."

Sabrina stared across the table at me, her eyes assessing my level of seriousness—and drunkenness—for a long torturous minute. She let out a sigh of resignation. "Fine. But one dance first." She hopped down from her stool and yanked me off mine, dragging me through the crowd. She grabbed two guys we'd talked to earlier from their table and pulled them with us onto the dance floor. She wasted no time grinding into her dark-haired dance partner, leaving the tall blond for me.

Dance music filled the bar, the bass much louder than I was used to at the local honky-tonk back home. But I let the liquor flowing through my veins move my hips—or maybe that was just my dance partner who'd grabbed hold of them and moved along with me.

Sabrina and I spent the next hour out on the dance floor. Sometimes we switched partners, sometimes I danced with Sabrina. All I knew was I laughed and had fun. Caden was there somewhere, but I didn't care. Why would I? My fun didn't depend on him. It depended on me. And for the first time in a long time, I was fine just being me.

Caden

"Dude. Just go out there."

My eyes jumped from the dance floor to Forester sitting across from me. "What?"

"You haven't heard a word I said all night."

"That's normal. I usually just tune you out."

He laughed and I could see the girls around us getting ready to swarm. Once it hit midnight, girls garnered their nerve and the quiet ones became forward and clingy. Two things I was in no mood for.

My eyes moved back to Finlay on the dance floor. I'd never seen her that carefree. The way her body moved to the music had me mesmerized. More than once I fought the urge to go grab the guys who were dancing all up in her space and tear their hands off her hips. Then I remembered I didn't have the right to do that. But had their hands roamed elsewhere, or had Finlay bent and started grinding her ass all over them, I would've stepped in. Because that wasn't her. The girl I knew, no matter how sassy she could get, had boundaries. And, regardless of whether or not we were on speaking terms, I wouldn't let her go there.

"You're both so fucking stubborn," Forester said, tearing my attention from Finlay.

"So, now you talk to her?"

"Dude. She's a sweet girl. Anyone can see that. Except you."

"She lied."

His pretty boy face twisted in disbelief. "So what? I lie to you all the time."

My head reeled back. "You do?"

He nodded. "When you ask me where I've been."

"Why?"

"Because I can. Because no one needs to know everything about me. Just like no one needs to know everything about you. Or Finlay."

His statements were valid. So why couldn't I just swallow my pride and apologize for the way things went down?

"And for the record, you sounded like an asshole in the locker room. She deserved better than that."

I dragged my fingers through my hair. "What am I supposed to do about it now?"

He tipped back his beer. When he finished, he wiped his mouth with his arm. "The opposite of what you've been doing."

Forester was the last one I expected a lecture from. But there I sat, being schooled by my own roommate.

After what felt like hours, Finlay and her friend stepped off the dance floor, all flushed and giddy. They linked arms like drunk girls usually did and staggered toward the door with the two guys trailing behind them.

"Make sure they get home all right," I said to Forester who'd already spotted them and jumped to his feet, moving to the door and slipping outside. Knowing him, he probably planned to get her friend's number.

I sat there milking my beer. One of many I'd downed over the past hour watching the girl I let walk out of my life—the girl I pushed out of my life—go wild on the dance floor. I'd set her loose. I'd ended things. So why the hell did I care who she went home with? A cacophony of voices swirled in my brain. Grady's. Forester's. Leslie's. Their words mixed with the jealousy brought on by Finlay having fun without me—despite me—taunted me. She clearly didn't need me. But did I need her?

Forester returned a few minutes later wearing a smug grin, having definitely scored her friend's number.

"Did they get home alright?"

"Don't you mean alone?"

I stared him down, in no mood to fuck around.

He slid into his seat. "They're on their way home in an Uber. *Alone.*"

A relieved breath whooshed through my lips.

He shook his head. "Makes no sense. You could be goin' home with her right now if you weren't so damn proud."

"You don't know Finlay like I do."

Forester rolled his eyes. "Exactly."

* * *

With a cotton mouth and a throbbing thigh, I jogged to the sideline during practice. I didn't dare complain about my recovering thigh or Coach would've questioned my ability to get it done. So I did what I always did when faced with a shitty situation. I dealt with it.

Speaking of shitty situations.

Finlay stood by the bench with a water bottle in each hand. I walked toward her with my hand extended. She stared me down, the hate in her eyes speaking volumes. Never one to back down, I held her stare. But she conceded faster than expected, placing a bottle down on the bench and walking to the other end of the sideline. Either she was feeling as hungover as me, or she just wanted nothing to do with me.

After practice, I slipped on my sneakers and grabbed my bag from my locker. When I stood to head out, Finlay walked out of the back room with her backpack on her back.

"Hey, I'll walk out with you," I said, surprising myself as much as I'd clearly surprised her.

She stopped dead in her tracks and turned to glare at me. "What about our last conversation didn't you understand?"

Okay. So I needed a different approach. "I saw you last night."

She lifted a shoulder. "So?"

"So, it looked like you were having a good time."

Her eyes narrowed. "What do you want, Brooks?"

Brooks? When the hell did she go back to calling me Brooks? "I'm not with Leslie."

"I don't care." Given her disgusted glare, she didn't.

I was single-handedly blowing it with every word out of my mouth. "I just thought you should know."

"The only thing I want to know is when I'm getting my jersey back."

Ouch. "It's at my house. Come by any time."

She scoffed. "I was shown the door. No need to revisit that stellar moment."

The pit in my stomach grew exponentially. *I'd* done this. *I'd* pushed her away. And as much as I blamed her for being dishonest with me, this ending badly was all me. "I was hurt."

"Funny." The chill in her voice was such a contrast to the Finlay I knew. "I felt nothing."

"That's enough," a deep voice demanded.

Our eyes shot to Coach Burns who stood in the doorway of his office. "Goodbye, Finlay," he said.

She spun away and walked out, not giving either of us a second glance.

Coach's eyes shot to mine, narrowed and pissed. "In my office."

I dragged myself into his office. He slammed the door behind me and sat down at his desk. A wall filled with team pictures of the fifteen teams he'd coached sat behind him. "Sit."

I dropped into the chair opposite him.

"What the fuck was that?"

"What?"

"Don't fuck with me, Brooks. What the hell is going on with you and Finlay?"

I shrugged.

"That doesn't answer my question."

"Didn't think you cared about my sex life."

His eyes darkened and a low growl formed in the back of his throat. Oh, fuck. I gripped the armrests, braced for him to lunge across the desk and put me through the wall. "Come again?"

I shook my head. "Nothing. Nothing's going on with me and Finlay."

His eyes stayed on mine for an alarmingly long time. "That's not what it looked like out there."

"Yeah, well. Looks can be deceiving."

He scrubbed both hands down his face, clearly annoyed to be having this conversation with me. "I warned you to take it easy on her. Isn't it obvious she's had it tough since losing Cole?"

I stared at him. "You knew they dated?"

His face scrunched until his eyes had almost disappeared. "Dated?"

I nodded.

Abruptly, he spun in his chair, reached up, and pulled a team picture off the wall. It was the picture from my freshman year. Coach handed it to me. "Look at him."

I didn't reach for the picture. "I remember what he looked like."

He pushed the picture forward. "I said look at the damn picture."

I begrudgingly took it, bringing it closer to my face. My eyes scanned the team. Though it had only been two years, those who still played looked so much younger.

"Look at Cole," he ordered.

I reluctantly dragged my eyes down to where he knelt right beside me. His big smile was so telling. All he'd ever wanted to do was play for Alabama. And there he was. So anxious for our first game. But that game never came for him.

"Notice anything?"

I glanced up at Coach. Impatience brimmed in his eyes. "What?"

"Look closely."

"Coach. You're not making any sense."

That's when it hit me. Same dark hair. Same green eyes. Same freckles dusting his nose.

Holy shit.

I looked up at Coach with what could only be described as horror on my face.

His only reply was a nod.

CHAPTER NINETEEN

Caden

"Finlay. Please open the door," I said, pounding on her door.

Two girls passed by, staring at me like I was a lunatic.

Who could blame them? I pretty much looked like one. But I wasn't used to feeling like I screwed up the best thing that ever happened to me. I pounded again, this time harder. The dull sound echoed down the hallway. "Come on, Finlay. Talk to me."

"She's not in there." Finlay's roommate walked toward me.

My shoulders dropped in defeat. I needed to make it right. I needed to see her to make it right.

"I take it you finally realized you were being an asshole?" she said, as if she could give two shits about who I was.

"Excuse me?"

"You're an asshole. I'm guessing you finally figured that out."

My eyes narrowed as she brushed by me and unlocked the door to their room.

I didn't budge as she stepped inside. My eyes swept over the super clean room I'd never gotten the chance to see. The cork board filled with the pictures of Cole and Finlay was there for anyone to see. She had nothing to hide. It was me who hadn't realized that. "Do you know where she is?"

She turned to face me still standing in the doorway, her arms folded across her chest. "Even if I did, I wouldn't tell you."

"I deserve that."

"Yup. You do."

"So, what'll it take?"

Her eyes lifted to the ceiling, taking her time and milking my desperation for all she could. "Why?"

My forehead scrunched. "Why what?"

"Why are you here now? What's changed?"

I took a deep breath and walked inside. I could tell by her fierce attitude, the one that probably gave lots of guys a run for their money, that it was gonna take some time to convince her.

* * *

I jogged down to the stadium an hour later. The sun had already set as I knocked on the locked door. Arnie, the night security guard, was good at looking the other way when me and some of the other guys wanted access to the field after hours. I heard the door unlocking before it cracked open and Arnie peeked out.

"She here?" I asked, winded from my run from her dorm.

He nodded.

I made it down to the sideline, out of breath and nervous as hell. I stopped. My eyes shot around, sweeping slowly over the field shrouded in darkness. A shadow in the center of the field caught my eye. I squinted until my eyes adjusted and all I could see was her silhouette.

With my nerves in my throat choking me with regret, I stepped out onto the grass. Finlay's perfect image came into focus the closer I got. She lay on her back staring up at the sky. "This spot taken?" I asked lamely as I stopped beside her.

She didn't look at me. "It's your field."

Even though I knew I deserved it, her cold tone still slayed me. I sat down beside her, keeping my distance so she didn't surprise me with a right hook. "I was an idiot."

She said nothing.

"I should have talked to you before jumping to conclusions."

I hated her silence, but I'd use it to my benefit.

"I guess that's something else we have in common. People jumping to conclusions about us," I said. "But the difference is you didn't when it came to me. You asked about the draft. You didn't just assume you knew what I'd do. I should've done the same for you. I should've heard you out." I looked to her, but her eyes remained on the sky. "I know Cole was your brother."

"It doesn't matter."

"Like hell it doesn't." I watched as she closed her eyes. "I'm sure you had your reasons for not telling me, Finlay. But I wish you had."

A humorless laugh broke through her lips. "You mean when you were kicking me out of your house? Should I have unloaded everything on you right then and there? I don't think so."

"I screwed up. And I'm sorry."

She scoffed.

"If I could take it all back, I would. I don't want to be the guy who hurts you, Finlay. I want to be the one who lifts you up. The one you want when you're sad and need comfort. The one you want when you're happy and need to share it with someone. I don't want to be the one who makes you sad. It's the last thing I want to do."

"Well, you did a pretty good job of it, didn't you?"

I deserved that. I guess I deserved a hell of a lot more than just that. So I gave her time, waiting for her to say what she'd been stewing over the entire time I'd been sitting there. Hell, since I'd pushed her away.

"I thought you knew me," she said after a long pause. "But then you went and completely blew it. And for what? What did you think I was trying to do?"

I shook my head. "You didn't even tell me your real last name."

"You never asked for my last name. Grace is my middle name."

"Come on, Finlay. Can't you see why I felt blindsided? Can't you see why I was confused by everything I found out. I had no idea how to make sense of it all. In the end it all came down to me feeling like you weren't being real with me."

She sat up, suddenly determined to look me in the eyes. "When? When I was beside you in your hospital bed? When I drove you all the way back here from Arkansas? When I slept with you?"

I dragged my fingers through my hair, realizing I was making everything worse and I didn't know how to salvage it. "I fucked up. But I told you. Girls do some messed up shit to get close to me. They see dollar signs when they look in my eyes. They see the notoriety of being with the starting quarterback. I just never know who to trust."

"Well, that's too bad. Because I saw none of that when I looked into your eyes. I just saw you."

Well, fuck me.

A distant siren pierced the silence as we stared at each other. What could I possibly say? Because I believed her. I'd always believed her. I had no reason not to. Until Leslie got into my head, making me question every damn thing. I should've gone with my own feelings. I should've gone with what I knew to be the truth. I was such an idiot.

After more silence passed between us, Finlay sucked in a deep breath and avoided my gaze. "For the last two years, I could barely get out of bed."

My gut clenched. I hated myself. I didn't deserve Finlay. And she didn't deserve the pain she'd been through. Or the pain I'd caused her.

"The only reason I'm here is because Coach came to my house and practically forced me to work for him. It was the only way to start picking up the pieces of my life. Come here and do what Cole never got the chance to do."

I was an asshole. A complete fucking asshole. "Finlay, I—"

"Then I see you. *You.* A guy I hated more than anyone."

My face scrunched. "What?"

"I remember you from Cole's wake."

"You do?" I didn't mean to sound so hopeful. But I did. It was strange she remembered me because I only remembered the blonde with bloodshot green eyes. All the sadness and heartache in them haunted me. They certainly weren't the same eyes I saw when I looked at

Finlay. Her eyes held something else. Determination. Purpose. Something that made it impossible to connect her to that girl at the wake. "You barely even looked at me."

"I saw you outside. You were smiling." Her voice cracked with emotion. "How could you smile?"

It was as if I'd been sucker-punched by her words. By her accusation. "What?"

The moonlight reflected off the tears pooling in her eyes. "When you walked away from the funeral home, someone patted you on the shoulder and you laughed and bumped his fist."

I blinked hard, my mind reeling back to that awful day. "Is that what you think?"

"I think you were happy you were getting your big break. With Cole out of the way, you were the starting quarterback."

My fists clenched the grass at my sides, shredding it to bits. "Are you fucking kidding me? If I didn't like you so much, I would seriously hate you right now," I growled.

"Tell me I'm wrong," she challenged, her shoulders pulling back in defiance.

I grabbed them more roughly than I should have, shaking her as I leveled her with my eyes. "You couldn't be more wrong."

"Prove it."

I couldn't get the words out fast enough. "Cole was my first friend here. He and I spent every day together that first month. He was an awesome guy. Funny. Athletic. Cocky. He was someone I just wanted to be around."

She closed her eyes and shook her head, like she couldn't bear to hear it.

"When he died, it destroyed me. I know we didn't know each other long, but we bonded. Just like you and me."

Even with her eyes closed, I could see the pain on her face. "Were you here…when it happened?"

A chill ran through me, wishing that day could forever be erased from my memory. "I was."

Her eyes opened as tears trailed down her cheeks. "Was he…in pain?"

I shook my head, finding the words difficult to conjure with her eyes on me and her bottom lip quivering. "No. It happened fast." My voice cracked with emotion. "I was with him, Finlay. He wasn't alone."

She nodded, but I knew that wasn't enough to comfort her or give her the closure she clearly needed.

"He talked about you all the time. Told me lots of old stories about the two of you and all the trouble you got into."

A sad smile touched her lips, fading just as quickly. "Did he tell you what an awful sister I turned out to be?"

I paused, knowing enough to tread lightly. "He just said the two of you hadn't spoken, like really spoken, in a long time."

Tears continued to trail down her cheeks. "I was so sick of living in his shadow." Her voice came out so small, so ashamed. "So I pushed him away."

I hurt for her, and for the regret she must've felt every day for leaving things unresolved with Cole. "I knew it had to be something like that. Especially since he smiled every time he talked about you."

"He did?" she asked through her tears.

I nodded. "I told him to email you. You know, let you know what he was feeling. But he was old school and wrote you the letter instead."

She could hardly speak. "What letter?"

My head retracted. "You didn't read it?"

She shook her head. "I didn't know."

I closed my eyes, mentally berating myself for wussing out that day. "It's why I was smiling. I planned on handing it to you at the wake, but there were so many people and you were in so much pain. I knew it wasn't the right time. But I saw you stuff a tissue into a pocket in your dress. So when Coach hugged you, I slipped it into your pocket."

"You did?"

I nodded. "I figured you'd find it when you were alone. Forester only congratulated me outside because he knew I'd gotten you Cole's letter."

Her eyes were wild, the thought of an unread letter from her dead brother stunning her silent. But did she still have the dress? I watched as she racked her brain, likely considering the same question.

"Do you still have the dress?"

She nodded as she pushed herself to her knees, ready to stand. "I've gotta get home. I've gotta read it."

"Finlay, it's late."

She stopped, her shoulders dropping before she sank back down onto the grass, clearly realizing she didn't have a car and couldn't get it right then. I hated that I didn't have the letter to give to her. She deserved to have it. She deserved to find closure.

"That's why you were always so hot and cold with me," I said, realization hitting me for the first time. "You thought I was happy Cole was gone."

Her lips twisted regrettably. "I wanted you to be this awful guy. I wanted to hate you, but then you kept giving me reasons not to…at least until a few weeks ago."

"I'm so sorry." The words were completely inadequate, especially given the apology I owed her.

"I've spent a lot of time hating you."

I lifted my thumbs to her cheeks to wipe away her tears, but she pulled back, wiping her own cheeks. "I'm sorry I keep giving you reason to. Cole was an awesome guy. You two are so much alike."

She scoffed through her tears.

"I'm serious. I don't know how I didn't make the connection. Both of you know your Alabama trivia. You're both smart asses. Even your looks are so similar." She said nothing, which not only sucked, but also made me wonder if I'd pissed her off more. All I knew was I couldn't bear the thought of her hating me any longer. "Forgive me. Give me another chance. Give us another chance."

She paused for a long time, her eyes following her hand as it brushed over the grass at her side. "Is that a challenge or a question?" she asked humorlessly.

"It's me telling you I screwed up. It's me saying you're the best thing that's come into my life in a long damn time. It's me admitting I was wrong." I watched as she considered my words and what they meant for us. Unfortunately, she looked unconvinced. "What do you say, Finlay?"

"I'm gonna need time."

"Okay. How much?"

She shrugged.

I wished she hadn't. I wanted her to look past it. I wanted her to forgive me right there and then. But I didn't want to risk everything by pushing her to decide. Especially now that I knew how much time she'd spent hating me. I stood up and held my hand out for her. "Come on. Let me walk you home."

She didn't grab my hand as she stood. I wouldn't lie. It hurt. But then again, it wouldn't have been my stubborn girl if she'd grabbed it.

As we made the short walk up the dark path from the stadium to her dorm in silence, I racked my brain for something to talk about—something to break the uncomfortable silence that had descended. But in the end, I only risked reminding her why she shouldn't forgive me if I said anything.

At the entrance to her dorm, she scanned her key card and pulled open the door. "See you at practice," she said, her eyes cutting over her shoulder for a brief moment before she walked inside.

She was breaking my heart by walking away from me. By not forgiving me. I knew I screwed up and didn't deserve her forgiveness, but it still sucked. The door behind her began to close slowly. I jammed my foot in, stopping it and pulling it back open. "Let me drive you home tomorrow."

Finlay spun around. "What?"

"I want to be there when you read the letter."

She stared at me, her eyes searching my face. "Why?"

"Because, I want to be there for you."

She gnawed on her bottom lip for a long time, her eyes studying the pattern on the tile floor. "I don't know."

I walked to her, grabbing her hands and rubbing my thumbs over the tops of them. She didn't pull them away, which gave me a sliver of hope. "Let me do whatever it takes to make this right."

She closed her eyes, visibly pained by my words and the hurt I'd caused her. "You've got practice."

"So do you. We can go as soon as it's over."

Her eyes opened, drifting while her mind undoubtedly searched for another excuse. "Can I let you know?"

I wanted to say no. I wanted to plead my case. But that hadn't worked so far. It wouldn't be easy getting back to where we left off. After believing lies, forgiveness wasn't easy. Neither was shedding anger that accompanied a betrayal like mine. So I did the only thing I could in that moment. I nodded.

Finlay's lips twisted again as she turned away from me.

"Finlay," I called.

She glanced over her shoulder.

"I'm sorry about Cole."

She nodded. "Me too." She retreated down the hallway and disappeared around the corner.

I walked out of her dorm and started up the path toward my house. Except for a few lights scattered amongst the dorms, darkness covered the campus. It was quite a contrast to the lively atmosphere during the day. But I much preferred the slow pace, especially when my head was so messed up from the night's events. How could I have not made the connection between Cole and Finlay? Sure, I hadn't known her real last name, but looking at that team picture—looking at her—I could see so many of their similarities.

I guess there was a lot Finlay and I didn't know about each other, but that didn't negate the fact that we were a perfect match. Even more so now that we shared Cole. That connection alone had to mean something.

Ten minutes into my trek home, my phone vibrated in my pocket. I slipped it out. A text from Finlay lit up my screen.

Okay.

I stopped dead in my tracks and closed my eyes, letting my head fall forward with relief. That one word meant so much more than I ever thought possible. It meant I could go home with her. It meant she hadn't written me off completely. And it meant there was still hope for us.

I looked up to the night sky, now overcast and starless. "I won't screw this up, Cole. You have my word. I'll treat her right."

And I would.

As long as she'd have me.

CHAPTER TWENTY

Finlay

I glanced over at Caden driving his truck, all countrified in his white T-shirt and cargo shorts. All he needed was the plaid shirt. He looked so comfortable behind the wheel. Then again, he would've looked just as comfortable driving a Porsche.

The foolish girl in me wanted to forgive him. Wanted to believe everything could remain in the past and this moment could be the future. Wanted to believe we'd both believed lies which in a messed-up sort of way made us even. But my rational side had nagging doubts, taunting me, making me wonder if he'd bail when the going got tough. I mean, isn't that what he'd already done? Isn't that what his dad had done to him?

His eyes cut to mine. "What are you looking at?"

Despite what happened because I hadn't been open with him, I still shrugged.

"Well, with your eyes glued to the side of my face, I'd say you were looking at me."

I smiled sadly, wondering if my hard feelings would dissipate the more time I spent with him. That's partially why I agreed to let him come home with me. To see if there was a chance I could get over it. That, and Sabrina stole my phone and texted him *Okay* before I could pull the phone out of her hands. "Oh, you noticed that?"

"How could I not? You're hot as hell."

I glanced out the window, eyeing the familiar back roads I'd grown up on. My nerves were definitely at an all-time high as we drove closer to my house. Not only because Caden was there hoping for my forgiveness, but because I was beyond anxious to see Cole's words. The letter had to be there. I hadn't looked at that dress since tearing it off after the wake and stuffing it in the furthest corner of my closet. I just needed to get to it. I just needed to hold the letter in my hand.

I'd called my parents to let them know I was stopping home—omitting the reason why in case it went terribly wrong. They'd promised to hurry home from my aunt's in Georgia, but I told them I'd stick around until they returned.

I pointed to a road approaching on our right. "It's that one."

Caden turned onto the dirt road, all twisty and bumpy, the way you'd expect out in the sticks of Alabama. I hadn't realized how much I missed simple things like that until the truck bounced around and dirt clouded up around us.

Caden laughed as the truck continued to spring up and down until the road finally leveled out in front of my house. He parked the truck and killed the engine.

I stared at the porch wrapped around the front of our old farmhouse. The white picket fence surrounding the large front yard. The gate at the side that Cole and I had broken too many times to count. The colorful flowers hanging from the window boxes and filling my mother's beds. It had been some time since I'd appreciated the home where I'd grown up. The last two years had been spent cursing its emptiness. But in that moment, with the smell of home filling my breaths, a sort of calm swept over me.

"You ready?" Caden asked.

I shook my head, needing another minute.

He slid his hand across the bench seat, placing it on top of mine. "Take all the time you need."

I nodded, knowing his words carried double meaning. I *would* take my time. With him. And with the letter that awaited me upstairs. Because as anxious as I was to read it, as soon as I did, it would be the last time Cole spoke to me. And I wasn't ready for that.

"Cole told me about the tire out back," Caden said, having no trouble talking about Cole as his voice pulled me out of my head. "Is it still there?"

The mention of Cole's name and his beloved tire in such a casual way lightened my anxiety. I wondered if that was Cole urging me to let Caden in. To forgive him. To give us another chance. Because in that moment, I loved knowing Caden knew Cole. I loved knowing we shared that. "Yeah."

"Can I see it?"

I nodded.

"Whenever you're ready, Finlay. No rush."

I grabbed the door handle and pushed open my door, not wanting to prolong it any longer. I slipped my hand out from beneath Caden's and hopped out. I didn't look back, but heard the driver's side door open then close. Caden's footsteps neared until he placed his hand on the small of my back. The small gesture eased my mind, urging me to take him around to the backyard. Caden didn't say a word, just followed alongside as we stepped through the gate and into the backyard. I stopped. The swing hung as it had in August, unused and swaying. The old football nearby made me wonder if my dad had used it, looking to bring some normalcy back to our home.

"Wait here." My feet carried me to the worn ball and I picked it up. I took a deep breath then turned to Caden, tossing him a perfect spiral, just like Cole taught me.

Caden caught it with ease. "Nice pass."

I motioned to the tire with my chin. "Give it a try."

His eyes narrowed on the tire swaying slightly from side to side. "You sure?"

I nodded. "Cole would've challenged you if he were here."

He nodded, a small smile quirking his lips. He took a couple steps to his left so he stood opposite the tire, eyeing it for a long time. I visualized Cole doing the same as he worked to perfect his passes over the years. Caden pulled back his throwing arm and released the ball. His spiral rebounded off the side of the tire, bouncing onto the lawn.

"Cole never had any trouble," I teased, leaning down and picking up the ball, spinning it in my hands as I stood. "You want another try?"

He shook his head, his eyes fixed on mine as he moved closer. He didn't stop until he stood in front of me and stared down into my eyes. "Come here." He slipped his hand into mine and I let him guide me to the tire. "Get on."

"I don't know if it can hold me."

With his free hand, he grabbed hold of the thick rope that held the tire to the tree and tugged down on it. The branch barely moved. "It's fine."

"I've never used it as a swing."

He shrugged. "So? I think it's time we made a new memory out here."

A ripple rolled through my belly. Sometimes he just knew the right thing to say at just the right moment. Other times I wanted to strangle him for his stupidity.

His presence at my house was definitely overwhelming, not to mention confusing. But I was trying to move forward. I truly was. The difference between the old me and the new me was the new me was capable of forgiveness. She didn't hold grudges. She acknowledged that not everyone had ulterior motives. At least, that's what she was trying to do. Because if I'd learned nothing from the way I left things with Cole, not only would it have been shameful, but it would have been a waste of time to stay angry. And clearly, time was a precious thing, not to be wasted on trivial, meaningless grudges.

"Okay." I released Caden's hand and stepped through the tire, sitting on the edge and wrapping my arms around it, hoping it would actually hold my weight.

He moved behind me, gently pushing my back. I lifted my feet, making it easier to soar. As I moved back and forth with the motion of the swing, the scent of my mother's flower beds swirled in the air. It was a smell I hadn't noticed anymore after Cole died. The world had become dull and lifeless. I barely stepped outside, hating the idea that I wouldn't find him out there practicing. But today, with Caden with me, knowing exactly what I needed in that moment, I could breathe.

"This is a lot easier than getting the ball through it."

I laughed. "See. That's why Cole would've challenged you. To make you look bad and him look good."

"He was a cocky bastard wasn't he?"

"Yup. I loved that about him." Tears welled in my eyes, and I didn't even try to stop them. "I wish I'd told him."

I couldn't see Caden's face, but I could hear the sympathy in his voice. "I'm sorry you lost him. And I'm sorry you have regrets."

"Yeah…It's like I've tried so hard to bottle them up that sometimes I think I might just explode from the weight of them."

"Doesn't sound like it's doing you any good."

"Clearly. I'm a wreck most of the time." It was much easier to admit with my back to him.

"Ever think of just saying what you feel? You know, getting those regrets off your chest."

"It's not that easy."

"Sure it is."

My eyes flicked over my shoulder. "Is that what you do?"

He grabbed hold of the tire and stopped it, twirling me around to face him. "I regret listening to Leslie."

My lips twisted, unsure what to say.

"I regret being apart from you."

I stared into his big blue eyes, searching for the truth in them.

"I regret hurting you. Because you are the last person in the world I want to hurt."

"Yeah? Why's that?"

"Because I'm falling for you, Finlay. Harder than I thought possible."

My heart thumped against my chest, his admission blowing any clear thoughts from my head. Our relationship thus far had been anything but easy, but his words just sounded so damn sincere.

His smile spread, as if just realizing what he'd admitted. "Didn't mean to spring that on you like that. I just saw the opportunity and went for it."

I swallowed around the sudden lump swelling in my throat. "So, you're serious?"

"Yup. And it felt damn good to get it off my chest."

I nodded, stunned by his sentiment after everything that had happened between us. "I'm gonna need some time to process that."

"How long?" His eyes held so much hope in that moment.

"I don't know."

He nodded. "I can handle that." He lifted my chin with his finger. "Especially if there's a chance you'll tell me you feel the same way."

The emotions he'd been eliciting in me couldn't be healthy. Great highs and even lower lows. Was that what falling in love was? Because, even though I wasn't naïve and expecting flowers and confessions of love at every turn, I expected it to be easier. "Are you thirsty?"

"A little," he said, skeptical of my sudden subject change.

I stepped out of the tire. "Come on. I've stalled long enough."

His brows arched as he grasped my arm to balance me. "You sure?"

"Nope."

I climbed the back steps and opened the door. People in the south still believed no one would break into their homes. The ingrained smell of my mom's homemade cooking filled the kitchen as we stepped inside. I walked to the refrigerator and pulled out a pitcher. "I hope you like sweet tea."

I placed the pitcher down on the counter and pulled two cups from the cupboard. Caden walked up behind me. I could feel the heat of him, his presence just as overwhelming here as it had been in the truck. But he didn't touch me. He knew better than to rush me. "You look good in the kitchen."

I glanced over my shoulder at him. "I'm not really the domestic type."

He placed his hands on my shoulders and spun me, backing me up against the counter so I needed to tip my head to look up at him. "Doesn't matter." He leaned down and, for a split second I thought he'd kiss my lips, but he pressed his lips to my forehead instead. "You're my type."

A gush of relief mixed with disappointment flooded me. "Thanks for coming home with me."

"You don't have to thank me. I wanted to be here," he assured me.

I nodded, my eyes sweeping over his features. God, he was so good looking—and in my kitchen hanging on every one of my words. "I just feel like I need to go up there alone."

Disappointment clouded his eyes. I knew he wanted to be there for me, but it was something I just needed to do alone. His disappointment transformed to understanding, as if he'd read my thoughts and wanted to give me what I needed. "Can I stay in the hallway? Just in case you need me?"

My heart drummed faster as I nodded, knowing I needed to get up there.

"Forget the drink. You can do this," he assured me.

I hoped his faith in me somehow made it true. I moved away from the counter and walked to the foot of the staircase, looking up at the menacing climb before me. I could do it. I could read the letter. I could hear what Cole really wanted to say to me. What he really thought of me.

I climbed the steps slowly, Caden's footsteps creaking behind me. When we reached the top landing, I pulled in a deep breath and walked to the door on the right. Things were exactly as Cole had left them. Nothing had been touched. His red Alabama comforter remained tightly pulled over his pillows. Football posters filled three walls. His trophies lined the shelves on the fourth.

Caden placed his hand gently on my shoulder as he stepped behind me. "He was this neat at school, too."

I scoffed. "Shocking. My mom picked up after his sloppy-ass most of the time."

Caden's laughter carried softly over my shoulder before tapering off. "Those are a lot of trophies."

"Did he tell you he started playing when he was four?"

"No."

"He was amazing even back then." I needed to keep moving before getting swept up in more memories of him. "Mine's the next one." I proceeded to my open door. My room was just as I'd left it. My teal comforter remained not nearly as tight as Cole's. Posters didn't line my walls, instead a purple tapestry hung behind my bed. My desk was cluttered and a few pictures of Cole and me were tucked into the side of my mirror.

"I'll wait here." Caden stepped away from my open door and leaned against the wall beside it, giving me the privacy I needed. "I hope you find what you're looking for."

I eyed him curiously. "You didn't read it?"

He shook his head. "What's in that letter's between you and Cole. I just stuck it in an envelope."

He easily could've read it. But even back then Caden respected Cole—and me—enough to let me be the only one to read my brother's private thoughts.

Some of the tension in my body released. Maybe Caden was the guy I thought he was. The guy I hoped he was. "Thank you."

He smiled. "Would you stop thanking me and get in there?"

I nodded, stepping slowly inside my bedroom. I hadn't been gone long, but things had changed. I had changed.

I walked to my closet and grasped the small knob on the wooden door, something I'd done thousands of times before. But at that moment, it felt like the hardest thing I'd ever had to do. I dragged in a deep breath and pulled open the door. Bare hangers hung amongst some sweaters I wouldn't need until winter break. I pushed them to the far right and reached into the left corner. The black dress hung as I'd left it, tucked far away. An unwanted reminder of that dreadful day.

Instead of pulling out the dress, I reached my hand into the pocket. Goosebumps raced across my skin when I grasped nothing but air. Panicked, I shoved my hand into the other pocket. My heart stuttered as my fingers grasped an envelope. Time stood still as I closed my eyes and clutched the envelope like it would disappear if I didn't hold it tightly enough. Eventually, I pulled it out and stared down at it as I moved to my bed, dropping slowly onto the edge.

For a long time I just stared at it, working up the nerve to actually reach inside and pull out the letter. I listened for Caden out in the hallway, but heard nothing but my heartbeat echoing in my ears and the low hum of the air conditioner down the hall in my parents' bedroom.

I braced myself before lifting the envelope's flap and pushing my fingers inside. The hair on the back of my neck stood as I pulled the folded paper from the inside. The single sheet became a brick in my hand. My eyes pricked with tears. My throat went dry. What if he didn't forgive me? What if he told me I was a selfish bitch? How could I live knowing what he really thought of me?

I closed my eyes, squeezing them tightly for a brief moment. When I opened them, my shaking hands unfolded the paper.

A shudder rushed up my spine at the sight of Cole's messy handwriting. I hadn't realized you could miss someone's handwriting. But I had. I'd missed everything about him.

I dragged in a long shaky breath. There was no going back.

Finlay,

My stubborn sister. My other half. My best friend. I miss you. I've missed you for the last year. Your goofy laugh. Your smile. Your witty comebacks. I've missed everything. And I blame myself. I'm your brother. I should've forced you to talk to me. Should've forced you to get over what was bothering you. Should've forced you to be my best friend again.

I know all the hype around me took its toll on you. How could it not? Eyes were on me when it was your senior year, too. But no one was asking where you were going to college. No one was offering you scholarships. No one wanted to interview you.

No one wanted to be around you for no other reason than you were going to be the starting quarterback for a big-name college and hopefully end up in the pros.

I never stopped to think about how my "celebrity" affected you. How it hurt you. It was only after getting here, and stepping back from the situation, that I got clarity. That I realized what happened between us.

Now don't think for one second you're blameless in this whole mess. You should've talked to me. You should've been honest instead of just being pissed off at me all the time. I didn't do anything wrong—except not realize what was going on with you.

Regardless of who was or wasn't at fault, I want you in my life again. The way you used to be. I want you to come visit me. I want you to be part of this new life I'm starting. I want you to meet my teammates and friends. Of course there are some douchebags on my team like Grady who thinks he's God's gift to the sport, but there are also some great ones, like my wide receiver Forester and my backup Brooks. Now don't get me wrong. Guys are guys and I'd never leave you alone with any of them, especially Brooks, but I want you to know him. I want you to know all of them.

As soon as I get the tickets for my first game, I'm sending two home to mom and dad and one to you at school with this letter so you can come sit in the front row. I can't think of anything that would make me prouder than to have you guys right where I can see you when I step out onto that field in crimson for the first time.

I wouldn't have made it here without you, Finlay. Don't think I don't know that. You're the one who played catch with me in the backyard until your arm was about to fall off. You were the one who let me tackle you into Mom's flower beds over and over again. You were the one who kept me grounded when all the attention could have gone to my head. You, Finlay, are the one I owe everything to. I will make the first move. I will make this better. All you have to do is meet me halfway. I love you, sis. And I want you back in my life.

Your handsome and humble older (by two minutes) brother,

Cole

Tears trailed down my cheeks as I lowered the letter to my lap. I could barely breathe as Cole's words hit the deepest part of my heart. The deepest part of my soul.

He understood.

He wanted to fix us.

He loved me.

I closed my eyes and fell back onto my bed, the mattress coils squeaking underneath me as I lay there with the letter clutched tightly to my chest. A welcome feeling of peace swept over me like a cool winter breeze for the first time in over two years.

After everything I'd done, after how rotten I'd been, he still wanted me to visit him. To know his friends. To come to his games. To love him.

"Are you okay?" Caden's voice trailed softly into my room. His footsteps neared, and the mattress dipped as he sat down beside me.

"He loved me," I said, almost unable to believe it myself.

"Of course he did. He wouldn't shut up about you."

I opened my eyes and handed Caden the letter. I wanted him to hear Cole's words. The ones he'd encouraged him to write.

"You sure?"

I nodded.

I lay there as he read the letter, feeling the pent-up guilt, regret, and sadness releasing from my body.

Caden laughed beside me, clearly getting to the part about him. "That son of a bitch."

I snickered. "I guess I need to stay away from you."

"Like hell you will." He laughed. "But I guess I would've given you the same advice if I were your brother. I kind of went a little wild freshman year." Caden finished reading the letter and placed it on my nightstand. He lay down beside me, rolling onto his side and facing me with his head resting in his palm. "He understood, Finlay. It took the distance to show him what was going on, but he knew the real you."

"I can't even believe it."

He ducked his head to capture my eyes. "Believe it."

I nodded, but there was still something I'd never get over, no matter how forgiven I was.

Caden searched my face. "What is it? What's wrong?"

"It just kills me to know he never got to play in a game. He worked so hard to get there. It just doesn't seem fair."

"It isn't fair." He lifted his fingers to my face, lightly brushing them over my damp cheek as his eyes bore into mine. They held regret and sorrow for my loss. "He—"

"Finlay? You here, honey?" my mom called from downstairs.

I jolted upright, wiping my damp eyes. "Shit."

Caden sat up beside me. "What?"

"I kind of neglected to mention you were bringing me home."

"So?"

"So they know how much I hate you."

"Hate-*ed*," he amended.

I rolled my eyes as I called out. "Be right down."

"Now be honest. You want to forgive me."

I cocked my head. Did I want to forgive him? Could I?

Seeing the indecision in my eyes, and probably worried he wouldn't like my response, he stood and reached for my hand. "Come on. Let's go get this introducing-me-to-the-parents thing out of the way."

I grabbed his hand and he pulled me to my feet before following me down the steps.

My parents stood at the bottom of the staircase, their eyes widening on Caden behind me.

"Hey," my dad said, realizing I'd just been upstairs with the hot football player I'd vowed to hate forever—*and* I'd been crying.

"You okay?" my mom asked, her weary eyes assessing my face.

I nodded. "Yeah."

Her eyes moved to Caden who'd stopped in front of them, even taller and broader standing in our small entryway. "You must be Caden."

"Yes, ma'am."

"Nice to meet you," my mom smiled warmly—because that's what southern women did. They'd ask questions once you were out of earshot.

I pulled her in for a hug and whispered, "Tell you everything later."

Caden turned to my father, extending his hand toward him. "Mr. Thatcher."

My dad had no choice but to shake his hand, though the thought of getting his shotgun and shooting the boy who just emerged from his daughter's bedroom seemed like a real possibility.

Keeping my dad calm and unarmed, I threw my arms around him and hugged him. "Everything's good," I whispered, before stepping back from him and standing beside Caden.

"Finlay let me tag along," Caden explained, probably sensing my dad's unease. "Hope you don't mind."

My parents shook their heads, both looking unsure what to make of the scene. Hell, I didn't know what to make of it myself. Last they heard there was nothing going on between me and Alabama's quarterback. And in reality, there wasn't. Caden drove me home. That was it. Unless you counted him admitting he was falling for me. Then there was that.

"I was a good friend of Cole's," he continued. "I'm sorry for your loss. I miss him too."

"Thank you," they said, their eyes casting down. It was my normal response to someone's sympathy as well.

"Cole never stopped talking about this place." Caden's eyes drifted around the main floor before settling back on my parents. "And all of you."

My mother trailed her finger under her eye, catching a solitary tear. "Oh, honey, thank you. It means a lot to hear that."

Caden shrugged like it was no big deal, but it was. He didn't have to say anything, but he did anyway. He glanced to me wearing a sad smile.

I looked to my dad. "He can't get it through the tire."

My dad laughed. "Big shot quarterback can't conquer the hole?"

I cringed. "Oh, Dad, bad analogy."

My dad glanced to my mom, like he didn't understand what he'd said. Out loud. In front of his daughter's…whatever Caden was to me.

"Woah," Caden interjected. "I only got one shot at the tire." He put extra emphasis on the word *tire*. "I'm sure I could do it if I had another shot."

I pointed toward the back door. "What's stopping you?"

Caden's eyes followed my finger. "Fine. Bring it."

"Sounds like we've got another cocky one," my dad said as he led the way outside.

"You have no idea. He and Cole are so similar." Now that I'd been forgiven, I felt like it was okay to talk freely about Cole.

My parents glanced to me, gauging my reaction to what I'd said.

I smiled, feeling good. Even having Caden there was proving to be better than expected.

We stepped out into the backyard. The sun had begun to set as my dad grabbed the ball and tossed it to Caden. Just like Cole, he caught it and took off running toward the edge of the lawn. Unlike Cole, he avoided my mom's flower beds. He turned and tossed it back to my dad like Cole had so many times before. My eyes stung as recollections of my brother playing in the backyard flooded me. I glanced to my mom and saw the same bittersweet memories reflected in her eyes.

The notion of moving on always seemed like leaving Cole behind. But maybe Caden had been right. Maybe we were just making new memories. And making new memories didn't mean replacing the old ones.

"Heads up, Finlay," my dad called as he tossed me the ball with a wide grin.

I caught it easily and glanced to Caden whose brows bounced like I knew they would, always surprised and impressed by my skills.

I took off running toward him, faking to the right, like I planned to run by him. He shuffled, grabbing me around my waist and lifting me right off the ground. I could hear my parents' laughter as I squealed. "Put me down."

He buried his nose in my neck and whispered. "If your parents weren't here, I'd drop you to the ground and show you how much I love being here with you."

Unexpected excitement bubbled in my stomach. *Shit.* The happiness Cole's letter had brought about almost caused me to forget the way Caden had treated me. The coldness in his eyes. In his words. Sure, I wanted to forget. I just didn't know if I could. "Then it's a good thing they're here."

He lowered me to my feet and stepped back, pulling the ball from my hands and tossing it to my dad.

"So let's see what you got," my dad teased as he threw him back the ball.

Caden caught it and aligned himself with the tire. He eyed the rubber target like he had earlier, pulling back his arm and releasing the ball. Again, it bounced off the side and landed on the ground.

My dad hissed and my mom laughed.

"Best of three," Caden pleaded.

My dad humored him, grabbing the ball and tossing it back to him.

Caden realigned himself. This time when he released a perfect spiral, it went right through the hole, bouncing on the grass behind it. He turned with a huge smile on his face, but we'd all gone silent. No one but Cole had ever gotten it through the tire that quickly.

Caden's smile fell when he realized we weren't celebrating.

The sad look in his eyes, and the emptiness I felt keeping him at arm's length, tugged at my heartstrings, waning my resolve. But a girl had to protect her heart. And Caden Brooks had the ability to break it twice. I wasn't sure I could handle that. But I also didn't want him feeling guilty—especially since he'd been the one to tell me about the letter. So I did what any foolish girl would do in that situation. I dropped my guard, running at him and throwing myself into his arms. Luckily he caught me, just as he stumbled back onto the lawn.

My parents' laughter filled the air as I lay on top of Caden in the middle of the lawn, cushioned by the soft grass beneath us. We gazed into each other's eyes. Caden's eyes softened in the corners and I could sense his relief and the hope that accompanied it.

"What do you say we hit Maxine's?" my dad interrupted, probably terrified we were about to make out in front of him.

"Maxine's?" Caden asked me.

"Country bar," I explained.

"I'm in," he called out to my dad.

"You sure? They'll make you dance," I warned him.

"You don't think this California guy can dance?"

"Line dance," I amended.

"Can't be that hard."

CHAPTER TWENTY-ONE

Finlay

"Shit," Caden cursed as he crashed into the man beside him as the group of dancers moved right and he moved left.

For someone so quick and agile on the field, he had absolutely no rhythm on the dance floor. It didn't seem to matter. The girls in the crowded bar loved every minute of him shaking his ass, regardless of how many innocent people he crashed into. Some approached our table during dinner to ask for selfies, and Caden handled it effortlessly, never forgetting where he was in the conversation with my parents when he finished with the fans. I wasn't the jealous type. But all the girls wrapping their arms around him for pictures brought on a jealous ache.

If I didn't get my head in check, the night had bad written all over it.

I could tell my parents liked him, asking him all about the team and his background without prying, especially when he mentioned he and his dad were estranged. After dinner, my parents ducked out, leaving the 'kids to their fun.' I wondered if it was their first trip back to Maxine's. Wondered if they'd been able to laugh and have fun like they'd been having with us all night.

On the dance floor, the music picked up, so did the steps. I laughed as I grabbed onto Caden's arm to bring him in the right direction as the host called out a new step.

"I suck," he said, looking from side to side at all the people who had every step perfected as they danced around us.

"You've never done it before," I assured him as my worn cowboy boots carried me to the left. "You just need practice."

"Does that mean you'll teach me?"

Why did everything he said have to sound so damn flirty? "If you play your cards right."

"Oh, fuck it." He turned to me in the middle of the dance floor and cupped my cheeks.

I stared up into his eyes as the colorful flashing lights reflected off his face and a popular country song serenaded us. My mind said pull away and make him work harder. My lips said let him kiss you.

"I'd much rather do this." His mouth slammed down on mine, making the decision for me. As the dancers continued around us and the music floated through the speakers, all I could focus on was Caden and the way his lips consumed mine. My body relaxed into him and I gave myself over to the kiss. His tongue dipped inside my mouth, softly stroking mine as his hands lowered from my cheeks and wrapped around my waist. He pulled me against his solid chest, showing me how he felt about being there with me. As much as I wanted to deny it, I felt the connection too. He was erasing the hesitation I'd felt for him, even just hours before. He was mesmerizing every part of my body.

Damn him.

Breathless and slightly dazed, I pulled back, my eyes scanning the crowded room. "People are staring."

"So what?"

I struggled to find the words. My head wanted me to slam on the brakes. But my racing heart wanted him all to myself.

"I was watching you," Caden said.

My eyes jumped back to his. "What?"

"At the bar. When you were dancing with Sabrina."

That night had been about me. About feeling free—or at least trying to—with him somewhere in the room.

"You looked so damn hot out there," he continued.

I swallowed hard, unable to tear my eyes away from his.

"I'd never felt so jealous in my entire life."

Huh?

"I wanted to kill those guys for putting their hands on my girl."

Oh, hell. "Let's get out of here," I said, unable to hold off any longer.

His smile spread as a devilish glint flashed in his eyes.

I wove through the people triple-stepping to my right and exited the dance floor with Caden's hands on my hips guiding me through the crowd. Within minutes, we reached his truck. He slipped into the driver's seat and I pointed the way, knowing exactly where I wanted to take him. The roads were dusty and winding as he sped through my small town.

"That was fun," Caden said, breaking the silence.

I burst out laughing as my eyes cut to his. "Seriously?"

He shrugged. "I got to hang with you. It's becoming my favorite thing to do."

"Oh yeah?"

"Oh, hell yeah," he said.

I threw back my head and laughed, finding it easier to fall back into our old banter with each passing minute. "More than football?"

"Damn close."

I rolled my eyes as I spotted the side road I'd been searching for. "Turn there," I said.

He turned onto it, stopping the truck only when he'd come to the dead end.

I eyed the wide wooded path to the right. "Can you make it?"

He didn't bother answering as he turned the truck onto the path, taking us off-roading, much to his delight. Through the trees, Maple Lake appeared under the full moon. No other cars were parked there. Caden's eyes took in the small lake as he parked beside it. "If I'm being completely honest here, my mind's having a field day right now."

"And?"

"And I'm hoping we're going skinny dipping"

I laughed. "Is that something you'd like to do?"

He laughed. "You don't ask a guy that. Of course I'd want you naked in a lake. Hell, I'd take you naked anywhere I can have you."

When the words left his lips, it was as if electricity zapped around the cab of the truck, bouncing off the windows, dashboard, and seat, with us in the center. Caden's eyes met mine. They were focused, narrowed, and sexy as hell. We were clearly in need of the same thing.

He slid his hand across the bench seat and grabbed mine, tugging me closer. I scooted over, feeling the heat of him everywhere. He leaned over and grasped my hips, lifting me so I straddled his lap. "That's better." My hands instinctively landed on his shoulders before slipping around his neck. He instantly buried his hands in my hair and pulled my mouth down to his. His kiss was anxious and forceful. His lips owned me. Hell, *he* owned me. Thanks to my sleeveless shirt, his hands moved over my bare shoulders and down my arms, slipping to the sides of my body and splaying at my hips, bracing me where I sat. Possessive and strong.

I didn't want him to stop kissing me. He'd ignited something in me. All his words—all his apologies—came flooding back. Reassuring me. Calming me.

Was that what forgiveness felt like?

Unable to get close enough, I shamelessly ground against the bulge in his jeans. He groaned into my mouth as his hands slipped under my top, coasting gently up my back. I'd almost forgotten how strong his hands were. How possessive. His thumbs brushed my bra strap. "Is this okay?" he asked against my lips.

"You'd be smart to shut up before I change my mind."

He wasted no time, unhooking my bra with the twist of his fingers. The straps slid down my shoulders but he didn't remove my shirt. My body tingled with anticipation. His hands coasted up and down my bare back in long strokes leaving a path of heat in their wake. He dropped his mouth to my neck, trailing a path of open-mouthed kisses along my skin. "I can't be responsible for my actions tonight," he assured me as he continued to press kisses to the skin beneath my ear. "I couldn't stop thinking about the way you threw that football. It was the hottest thing I've ever seen."

"Stop talking."

Without warning, he threw open his door and jumped out of the truck with me clutched to his front. He stalked along the truck to the back and unhitched the tailgate. The metal creaked in the quiet night as it dropped open. He sat me on the edge. "There's a blanket in the storage box."

I scooted back toward the cab, keeping him in my sights as I reached into the box. I pulled out the blanket and spread the soft material out in the bed of the truck.

With a predatory look in his eyes, Caden reached behind his neck, pulling his shirt over his head.

My breath hitched as he stood before me shirtless. The hunger in his eyes was undeniable. Though it was warm outside, goosebumps rushed up my arms and legs as he climbed into the bed of the truck and crept toward me. "Do you have any idea how amazing you are?"

My eyes stayed on his. "Yes."

His lips slid into a cocky smirk. "Of course you do."

"It's you who took so long to figure it out."

"Is that right?"

I nodded.

His smile faded, though his eyes remained focused on mine. "I'm so damn sorry I hurt you. But I hope you know, I was hurting myself worse by staying away."

I swallowed down the words I wanted to say. Because I earned this apology and all the others that came before.

"I was stupid and I promise I will never ever hurt you again."

I nodded, my heart racing something fierce.

His hands reached for the hem of my shirt. "Now, I'm going to take your clothes off and I'm going to show you just how sorry I am."

I shook my head, lifting my chin toward his jeans. "You first."

He laughed as he dropped my shirt and reached for the button on his jeans, slipping it through the slot and tugging his jeans down and over his feet. "This shouldn't be that impressive since you've already seen it. On second thought. Yes it should be."

I laughed as he grabbed a condom from his wallet then tossed his jeans into the corner of the truck bed, leaving him in his black boxer briefs. I nodded to the boxers. "I don't think you're finished."

He glanced up. "I'll show you mine if you show me yours."

"Has that line actually worked before?"

He shrugged in a way that told me it had. But he was there with me. Not Leslie or some other girl. Me. And—for the first time in weeks—I was so damn happy he was.

I grabbed hold of the hem of my shirt and peeled it up my skin, taking my loose bra with it. It wasn't like Caden hadn't seen me naked before. But knowing the darkness kept me somewhat concealed, I felt more comfortable stripping down. That—and his sharp intake of breath once my shirt cleared my head—did wonders for my ego.

"Are your parents gonna wonder where we are?" he asked.

"Are you seriously bringing up my parents right now?"

He smiled as he pushed off his boxers and lowered me onto my back on the blanket. He cradled my head with one hand and reached for his jeans, bunching them into a soft pile and placing them beneath my head as he covered me with his body. "You okay?"

"I am now."

He snickered. "Yeah, but I need you out of these cutoffs. Just leave on the hot boots."

I nodded, my belly a fluttery mess.

He rolled off of me and reached for my button. I didn't bother waiting, lifting my butt and dragging my shorts and underwear down my legs myself. Caden tugged them over my cowboy boots which were apparently staying on. His eyes drifted over my body sending a shudder rocking through me. "You're so hot."

"Is that all I am?"

He rolled on the condom, then lay back on top of me, his weight on his arms and his eyes zoned in on mine. I could feel his erection against my belly and every part of me tingled with anticipation. "Oh, babe, you are every one of my dreams come to life."

"Dreams change."

He shook his head. "Not this one."

I closed my eyes, the revelations of the day becoming far too much for me to bear any longer.

"Hey," he said softly.

I opened my eyes, unable to hide the tears glazing them.

"Is this okay? The truck? Us out here?"

I nodded. "It's perfect."

He smiled before his lips dropped to mine and his tongue plunged inside my mouth, aggressive and deep. His hips began to move, his length pressed low against me. I wrapped my arms around him, holding him to me as he lowered his hips, running his length over the wetness he'd created. Was he teasing me or prolonging the moment? It didn't matter. The moon was the only witness to us deep in the woods as he added pressure, pushing inside of me with one hard thrust. My back arched, my chest pushing into him as I groaned into the quiet night. His mouth captured my sounds as he sucked away at my tongue.

He kept a slow pace as he moved inside me, filling me and hitting the spots I yearned for him to hit. I bent my legs, cradling his hips, hoping to drive him even deeper. He moaned into my mouth, enjoying the easier access. I upped the ante, lifting my feet and crossing my boots behind his ass.

"You must be trying to kill me," he growled against my lips as his hips drove hard and fast, pounding away at me.

I tried to take it all in. Caden on top of me—inside me. His smooth skin. The squeaking of the truck. The night air on my bare skin.

Caden's lips dropped to my neck, his tongue tracing a path to my ear. His breathing was labored as he began sucking away at the sensitive skin there.

"Stay right there," I urged.

"Not goin' anywhere," he ground out against my neck.

I dug my fingers into his ass, loving the feel of it clenching as it moved back and forth. I craved the release only he could give me.

"I've missed being inside you."

"Stop."

His hips stopped moving.

I panicked. "No, not that."

He grunted a laugh as his hips surged deeper.

My head pushed into the jeans behind my head, my neck arching. "Don't you dare stop."

Caden focused. His thrusts became harder, grinding deeper. He reached down between us, running the pad of his thumb over the spot that sent my eyes rolling into the back of my head and ripples igniting.

"Oh, God."

"I'm right with you, Finlay."

I closed my eyes, concentrating on the feel of him moving in and out of me, the building sensations as he circled with his thumb, the slapping of our skin, the motion of the truck, the musky scent of his hair, and his heavy breaths. Then, as if we hadn't been apart, my insides shattered, tingling sensations flooding through every part of my body. I could hardly catch my breath as tiny tremors moved over me in an exhausting calm.

Caden continued his pursuit, thrusting a few more times before his body stilled and he groaned into my ear. I loved that sound. And the feel of him lowering down and relaxing on top of me, all sweaty and solid. There was something about having all of his weight on me. Something possessive and freeing. Something that told me he was mine.

"You know we're doing that again, right?"

I laughed.

He pulled back, lifting his weight onto his forearms and staring down at me with a seriousness in his eyes. "I'm glad I didn't meet you until this year," he said.

"Why's that?"

"I wouldn't have been ready for you."

"Oh no?"

He shook his head. "But I'm ready for you now."

I smiled as he pressed his sweaty forehead to mine. And in that moment, I knew it was the truth.

Caden

"What are the odds you'll win today?" Finlay asked from the passenger seat of my truck the following morning, her hot cowboy boots resting on the dashboard.

"If last night was any indication, things are definitely going my way," I assured her.

She smiled. She was so damn cute—and those cowboy boots were killing me. Scratch that. Picturing her in them and only them the previous night was killing me and keeping me hard. Normally, not a huge problem, but I had a game to play.

Her eyes drifted out the window as we passed yet another sign for school. A stark reminder we'd be returning to reality.

The silence in the truck became deafening. Was she having regrets? "What are you thinking?"

"A girl's allowed to have her secrets."

I laughed, feeling relieved by her calm response. "I guess that's fair." And it was. Because I had a secret of my own.

I pulled the truck up in front of my house and killed the engine.

"I've got to get to the dorm to shower," she said, obviously thinking I planned to kidnap her. If I didn't have a game, I probably would have.

I beckoned her over with my finger. "You can take my truck when I'm done with you."

She grinned as she scooted across the seat until her leg brushed mine.

I patted my hands on my lap, a request for her to straddle me like she had by the lake. She shook her head. I guess I didn't blame her. People were walking all around and both of us were on the verge of being late to the field house. "Fine."

She laughed. "You do realize you're pouting, right?"

"Football players don't pout," I said.

"I don't know about other football players, but you're definitely pouting."

I reached over and slipped my hand behind her head, tunneling my fingers through her hair and pulling her to me. My lips descended on hers, and I made damn sure not to release her until I was good and ready. It did nothing for the hard-on in my jeans, but I needed the reassurance that last night happened. That it changed everything between us. That it fixed what I'd broken. I tore my lips away, leaving her breathless and flushed. "Fuck that felt good."

She laughed. "Go. You've got a game to win."

"Trying to get rid of me already?"

She shoved at my arm, trying to give me a push, but it was gonna take a lot more than that to get me to leave her.

"You do realize I line danced for you, right?"

"That's what you called it?" she teased.

I grabbed both of her arms and pulled her onto my lap, earning me an adorable squeal. I linked my arms around her back so she couldn't escape. "This is exactly where I want you."

"What is it with us and vehicles?" she asked, her pretty face moving closer to mine until her lips hovered a mere breath away.

I smiled. "I don't think it's vehicles. I just think it's *us*. And I'd take you anywhere."

Finlay pressed her lips to mine, and it was all the confirmation I needed to know that she liked my answer. And she should. It was the truth.

CHAPTER TWENTY-TWO

Finlay

I filled my bottles at the sink in the locker room. I could hear Coach giving the guys a pep talk in the other room before they headed out for some pre-game warmups prior to the stadium gates opening.

"Finlay?"

I glanced over my shoulder.

Yvette stood there with a clipboard in her hand. "I was right, wasn't I?"

I smiled as visions of the previous night materialized.

"Thought so," she said as she turned away.

"Hey."

She stopped and glanced back over her shoulder.

"How about you and Grady?" I raised my brows quid pro quo.

She lifted a shoulder. "He's not as bad as he seems." With that, she turned and headed out to the field.

I stood there with my grin fixed in place. Maybe we weren't the two most likely couples on campus, but for whatever reason, we worked.

A little while later, I finished up with my bottles and rolled my cart down toward the stadium. Some of the guys were on their way back to get their uniforms on while the stadium filled with fans. Caden passed me with a knowing grin, but kept walking with Forester who gave me the same knowing look. What had Caden told him?

On the sideline, I organized my bottles on the table behind the bench. I glanced up to the seats, shocked to find my parents sitting nearby. I'd given them tickets, but they said they wouldn't be able to make it. They waved as soon as they spotted me. Sabrina sat beside them with Forester's number painted on her cheek.

Had I missed something?

I lifted my chin at Sabrina who shrugged coyly. I knew he'd gotten her number the night at the bar—after threatening our dance partners—but she hadn't mentioned he'd called. Oh. There was something there, and I couldn't wait to find out what it was.

The stadium filled quickly, and by the time the opponents took the field to boos from the home crowd, the place had filled to capacity. Our theme song blared and the entire stadium shook as the team ran onto the field clad in crimson and white, jumping around trying to hype up the already overzealous crowd.

I stopped to admire the scene for the first time in a long while the stadium roared around me. My eyes searched for Caden amongst the players on the field. But I couldn't find number twelve in all the madness.

It was then a shiver rolled up my spine and the hair on the back of my neck stood on end.

It couldn't be.

I blinked several times as my eyes welled and I stood frozen to my spot. Dumbstruck. Terrified. Confused. It was as if it was happening in slow motion. Number sixteen jogged over to me on the sideline, stopping in front of me. He grabbed his helmet with both hands and, for a split second, I expected it to be Cole. Once the helmet cleared his head, Caden stood there in Cole's jersey.

Tears spilled from my eyes. "What are you doing?"

"Cole's jersey deserved to be worn. He deserved to play."

I dropped my head and my shoulders shook as silent sobs tore out of me.

Caden wrapped his arms around me, enveloping me in Cole's jersey. "Oh, baby. I'm so sorry. I didn't mean to upset you."

I shook my head. "No. I'm happy." I pulled back enough to look up at him, meeting him with teary eyes. "I can't believe you did this for Cole."

He dropped his forehead to mine, his gaze never wavering. "I didn't do it for Cole. I did it for you. I did it for Finlay."

My entire being melted into him as I resisted the urge to slither down into a puddle of useless goo right there and then. But oh, how I wanted to. His sincerity—his grand gesture—absolutely floored me.

"I love you, Finlay. There's not a thing in this world I wouldn't do for you."

I closed my eyes, absorbing his words. His actions. His love. I'd found the right guy for me. A guy who loved my brother. A guy who loved me. My eyes fluttered open, lifting to the crimson sky as the sun began to lower in the distance. Cole was watching. I just knew he had everything to do with Caden and me getting together. I just knew it. "Then get out there and win the game."

He pressed his lips to mine. Everything about this kiss reassured me that this thing between us wasn't just a fling. This was something real. Something with the potential to withstand anything that got thrown in our way.

The sound of applause around us pulled me out of the kiss a lot sooner than I was ready for. When my eyes flashed around, the team stood clapping with big dumb smiles on their faces. I couldn't hide mine as I looked at all of them, the black paint under their eyes neatly lined for the time being. And for the first time, I saw true regret in their eyes. I guess the cat was out of the bag. I was Cole's sister. And for once they were looking *at me* and not through me. They respected me and my being there. Even Grady applauded, lifting his hands to his mouth and howling.

He was such an idiot.

I shot a glance over my shoulder at the crowded seats behind us. Leslie stood with her friends watching the entire scene. Tears trailed down her cheeks. Had she finally realized she'd made a huge mistake in telling Caden about Cole? *Or* had it just hit her that Caden was never going back to her? He was mine. And that felt so good to finally admit.

My eyes shifted from Leslie to my parents and Sabrina standing and clapping a section over.

"I asked them to come," Caden admitted.

My head swung back around. I stared into his pretty eyes, focused solely on me in that crowded stadium. "I love having you inside me."

His eyes widened, surprised by my candor.

I grabbed his hand and placed it over my heart. "Inside here, dirty mind."

Though the sound of his laughter was lost in the din of the crowd, I could feel the rumble of it beneath my hand and see it in the amused lines around his eyes. "I knew that."

EPILOGUE

Finlay

Two Years Later

My feet bounced as I sat in the front row of the sold out stadium. The Florida sun had been ruthless all afternoon, but as I clasped Caden's mother's hand beside me, we watched the play clock tick down to zero. When it flashed, we jumped to our feet with the rest of the Miami fans all clad in hues of teal and orange. Caden's first game in the pros had been a nail-biter. No one took it easy on the rookie quarterback, but he handled it with ease. Besides, it wasn't like he had guys like Grady on his line anymore. He was protected by guys paid millions to be out there, guys who breathed football and gave it their all on every play.

I watched proudly as Caden, along with a mob of photographers and cameramen in tow, jogged across the field and shook the opposing quarterback's hand. We'd watched games together on television over the past two years, and when the moment came for the quarterbacks to shake, I always felt a chill slither up my spine knowing someday that would be Caden out there. Now that day had come.

He turned and jogged toward the sideline with his helmet in his hand and his face flushed and sweaty. The pretty sideline reporter jogged over to him, stopping him for his first post-game interview.

Caden's eyes flashed around until he found our section, spotting us standing there smiling and bursting with excitement. A smile tipped his lips before he focused on the reporter.

His face appeared larger than life on the jumbo-tron as the interview was broadcast live in the stadium for the fans who'd yet to leave their seats.

"Congrats on your first of many wins, Caden," the reporter said, her voice reverberating throughout the massive space.

The crowd cheered, their roar filling the stadium.

Caden glanced around, taking it all in and trying to acknowledge each and every fan that came out to the game and welcomed him to their team. He glanced back to the reporter. "Thank you. I couldn't have done it without my teammates. These guys are the epitome of athleticism and hard work," he explained, a little winded from the last few plays of the game.

"Do you think having a rookie at the helm is something they appreciated today?" she asked.

"You might need to ask them," he laughed. "But I hope so."

The sound of his laughter, mixed with how damn hot he looked in that uniform, sent ripples of pleasure spreading through me.

"But I'm serious when I say I couldn't have done it alone," he continued. "It's truly a team effort here in

Miami. And have I mentioned these amazing fans?" His eyes jumped around the stadium.

The crowd erupted, the volume in the stadium ear-splitting.

Caden smiled as he glanced around. "They make it easier to do our jobs."

"So tell us, how's it feel to be playing so close to Alabama?"

"Amazing. I can't even begin to tell you how happy I am to be staying in the south. I've grown a real love for it over the last four years."

"Any big plans now that you're in Miami?"

He smiled a crooked smile that probably melted the panties off every woman in that stadium—*and* the ones watching at home. "I'm excited my mom's finally relocated here and that my fiancée moved in with me."

Fiancée? My face fell as my eyes shot from him on the jumbo-tron to him standing a hundred feet away.

"Thanks, Caden," the reporter said with a smile.

"Thanks," he said, already turning away from her.

"When were you going to tell me the good news?" Caden's mother asked, excitement filling her features.

I stared blankly at her, my mind spiraling. Had he misspoken? Had he been joking around? Sure, we'd moved in together after he got drafted and I enrolled in a nursing school nearby, but we'd never spoken about marriage before.

"After I asked her," Caden's voice traveled over to us.

Our heads shot to him, standing beneath us down on the sideline. My heart fluttered at the sight of him. I leaned over the railing, instinctively reaching for him. Somehow he lifted me over the railing and pulled me down to the sideline. When we stood on even ground, I stared up into his eyes as he grabbed my hands.

"Nothing about us has been conventional," he said, his eyes filled with so much love and admiration. "So I figured…" He dropped down onto his knee.

My eyes rounded as I pulled in a deep breath. This was really happening. This was really freaking happening. And even though thousands of people remained in the stadium, their voices became muted and all I could hear was the thumping of my heart.

"Finlay, you're the best thing that's ever happened to me. You love me and you love football. In my book that makes you perfect. Marry me."

Even as my eyes welled, laughter erupted from deep inside me. "I've hated you and loved you, both just as strongly. Loving you has definitely been easier."

His smile grew, so did the hope in his eyes.

"Cole wouldn't trust anyone else with me. Which is good because I can't see myself with anyone else. So, yes. Yes, I'll marry you."

Caden laughed, his relief and happiness evident as he stood, reaching up to his mom.

She shot me a conspiratorial grin before placing a ring into his opened palm. I shook my head. I should've known he'd have an accomplice.

Caden turned back to me. He grabbed my shaking hand and looked me in my teary eyes as he slid the ring onto my finger. I gazed down at the massive stone sparkling like nothing I'd ever seen before. But Caden gave me no more time to admire it. He tugged me against his chest and wrapped me in his arms. He pressed his lips to the top of my head. "I love you." After a long moment of feeling truly at peace in the arms I'd get to spend forever in, he pulled back to see my face. The sincerity in his eyes floored me, just as fiercely as the day I realized everything between us was getting complicated. "I don't think you understand just how much."

I nodded, because I felt it, too. "I do."

Caden had been placed in my life for a reason. Cole placed him there. All Cole would have wanted was for me to be happy. And Caden made me happy. Beyond happy.

And I could say with much certainty that he'd done a fine job working his way inside of me.

Oh, and my heart, too.

THE END

OTHER TITLES

For You Standalone Series

For Forester (Book #2 Trace's Story)

For Crosby (Book #3 Sabrina's Story)

For Emery (Book #4 Grady's Story)

Savage Beasts Rock Star Standalone Series

Kozart

Treyton

Standalones

I Just Need You

You're the Reason

Until Alex

Since Drew

Before Hadley

ACKNOWLEDGEMENTS

Thank you amazing readers for taking the time to read Finlay and Caden's story. I hope you enjoyed it as much as I enjoyed writing it!

To all the bloggers and readers who've spread the word about my books. Thank you so much! Self-publishing is truly a team effort and I would not be able to write and get my books out there without you! So thank you!!!!

To my wonderful beta readers: Dali, Kat, Neilliza, Megan D, and Kim. Thank you for your invaluable suggestions and for taking the time to help me. I appreciate it more than you could possibly know.

To the multi-talented (author and editor) Stephanie Elliot. Thank you for just being you. For all your encouragement. For your editing expertise. For giving me the push to begin this awesome journey. For pointing out all the times I write sentences like this. LOL!

To photographer Lindee Robinson. Thank you for giving me so many beautiful photos to choose from for the cover. I can't wait to see what you have for my next book.

And last, but certainly not least, to Letitia at RBA Designs. Thank you for creating yet another beautiful cover for me. You are so kind and patient and a true pleasure to work with.

ABOUT THE AUTHOR

J. Nathan resides on the east coast with her husband and six-year-old son. She is an avid reader of all things romance. Happy endings are a must. Alpha males with chips on their shoulders are an added bonus. When she's not curled up with a good book, she can be found spending time with family and friends and working on her next novel.

Made in the USA
Middletown, DE
18 May 2021

39960128R00151